MICHAEL ALLEN GEORGE

A REFUGE RESTORED

MARUGE
PUBLISHING

A REFUGE RESTORED

MICHAEL ALLEN GEORGE

For The Special Ones
Tom and Bonnie Haubenschild

Whatever it is, they always give it their all
Without them, life would be so much less

BOOKS BY
MICHAEL GEORGE AND/OR MICHAEL ALLEN GEORGE

THE REFUGE MYSTERY SERIES

Why A Refuge   Book One
Available by Michael George and Michael Allen George

THE FOLLOWING BY MICHAEL GEORGE

Bridge To No Good	Book Two
Grass Was Greener	Book Three
To Save The Refuge	Book Four
Without Refuge	Book Five
Refuge Of Another Kind	Book Six

THE REFUGE MYSTERY SERIES
WRITTEN AS MICHAEL ALLEN GEORGE

Bridge For A Lost Refuge	Book Two Also as Bridge To No Good
Places Of Refuge	Book Seven
Refuge Life And Home	Book Eight
Refuge Rescuers	Book Nine
Walking The Refuge	Book Ten
Lisa's Refuge	Book Eleven
Seeking Refuge	Book Twelve
A Refuge Banned	Book Thirteen
A Refuge Restored	Book Fourteen

BOOKS WRITTEN AS MICHAEL GEORGE

Horses Lemons And Pretty Girls
More Horses And Pretty Girls
Finding Peri Gray
Of Rain Barrels And Bridges
Books Written With Bud George
And David George
Stories From Three Brothers

MORE STORIES FROM THREE BROTHERS - AS MICHAEL ALLEN GEORGE

When ordering my books online it is best to capitalize title and author's name.
It is also best to use the Title of the book and the author's name.

PROLOGUE

By way of excessive aggression, Jerry Smith was leader of the group. Athletes all, they patrolled any and every place where young women alone could be found. They avoided couples. Husbands and boyfriends were sometimes defensive and that brought the chance of one of them being hurt. It wasn't the pain they worried about so much as it was the concern about a serious injury. That was something which could interfere with their hoped for athletic careers. They all played football.

It was midmorning on a late May day. An exceptional day for that time of the year in Minnesota. A place well known for its miserable and sometimes cruel weather that often lasted as long as seven months. This day was filled with sunshine, a warm mid-seventies temperature, and trees of several kinds blooming. Their leaves were just beginning to pop.

There were six young men cruising the parking lot of a medical clinic, in their oversized SUV, in a typical Minneapolis suburb. It was landscaped with shrubs, trees, and large areas of flowers. After they'd driven through nearly all of the various sections of the lot, they finally found what they were sure were good candidates to fulfill their desires.

There were two of them. A mother, who been told that morning by her doctor that she had breast cancer, and the daughter who had gone to the doctor with her mother, just in case the news they were there to learn was bad. Which it was.

The mother was only forty-two years old, and still carried the same beauty she had when she was only thirty. The daughter, now just twenty years old, was a beautiful brunette with a near perfect figure. Because of the exceptionally nice weather, both women were dressed simply, wearing cotton blouses and slacks.

They were close to their car when the six young men drove up. They were out of their SUV before the two women could react. They did, however, manage to scream as they were dragged by the men to their SUV.

The screams were heard by a couple in a pickup only two sections away. Bob Anderson, a retired dairy farmer, immediately drove toward the screams. He reached the section of the parking lot where the women were being abducted, just as they were being pushed into the athlete's SUV. He knew he had to do something to stop the men, but his options were limited. He turned to his wife, Beth.

"Call nine one one," he said. It was an unnecessary request. She was already waiting for an answer on her cell phone.

What Bob wanted to do at that point was to get out of his pickup and try to help the two women. The problem with that was the fact that he couldn't do it. His heart was bad, and because of that is physical condition was abysmal. He had deteriorated to the point that he required a cane to walk. His wife now had more physical strength than he did.

With no other way to stop them and no police in sight, Bob used the only option he had. He jammed the accelerator of his truck to the floor and slammed it into the right front quarter panel of the SUV. The collision folded the fender into the SUV's front wheel to the point it flattened the tire and made it impossible to move the steering wheel.

Four of the six men leaped out of the SUV, pulled Bob out of his pickup, and started to beat the hell out of him. Beth got out and rushed around to his side of the pickup to assist him. She had extensive defense training, so she managed to do some damage to a couple of the men before she was hit from behind. But before she was, her actions created enough chaos to allow the two women to escape the SUV. She fell to the ground from the blow, and lay there barely conscious as the men continued to lay into Bob.

He was unconscious when the police arrived. The six men were gone, but the two women were still free. The police were slow to look for the men, insisting that they needed to question the two women and Beth before they got bogged down in a search for men who might or might not be real. After all, there was no sense in going off on a wild goose chase if the three women couldn't give them the same story. Bob laying on the ground unconscious along with the damaged enough to be impossible to drive SUV at the scene, wasn't quite enough evidence for them to prove someone had been there.

Telling exactly the same story was something the three women couldn't do. Two women were inside the SUV when the fight started, and Beth was outside. She was only at the first part of the fight, then taken out of it by a blow to the back of her head. So it took the cops a while to get it together enough to go after the men. For them, it was a complicated story. By the time they could understand it, it was too late to make any attempt to find the would be abductors.

The SUV was reported stolen shortly after the police got to the scene of the attempted kidnapping. Since the registered owner of it was also the owner of the largest insurance agency in the state, and sat on that suburbs city council, the police were sure that the SUV had actually been stolen. They then assumed that the son of the insurance man, who was the star quarterback on the local high school football team, had nothing to do with what had just gone down. Never mind that the younger of the two women identified him when she was shown his photo on one of the cops cell phones. Star high school quarterbacks who were the son of one of the richest men in the city simply didn't go around abducting women. Everyone knew that they could get any woman they wanted. They were, after all, star football players.

An ambulance arrived while all that was going on, and without telling Beth what they were doing, they loaded Bob into it and hauled him to the hospital. By the time the police were done with her, Bob's pickup had been towed away to some unknown repair shop. At that point, things were so confused that the police were hesitant to tell Beth anything. At first they didn't even want to tell her which hospital Bob was taken to. According to them, she and Bob were now suspected of attacking the SUV without any reasonable cause. By then Beth could see that they were covering up for whomever it was that committed the crimes.

When they finally relented and told her some of what they were thinking, there was no longer any doubt about what they were doing. They refused to provide her a ride to the hospital or anywhere else. From their stated point of view, Bob and Beth were every bit a guilty of a crime as the men who performed the attempted abduction, if there were even any such men.

It was the two women who gave Beth a ride the hospital. They were clearly as upset about the police ignoring their explanations as she was. They, however, didn't have Beth's clear understanding of what was actually going on.

On the way there they thanked Beth, then introduced themselves. "I'm Melissa Carpenter," the older woman said. "And this is my daughter, Jane."

"I'm Beth, Beth Anderson. My husband, Bob, is the one who got beat up. His heart is bad. That's why he couldn't fight back. If he doesn't get a transplant soon, he's not going to make it. And from the beating he took he probably won't make it through this, so the transplant won't matter."

"I'm so sorry," the woman said. She then gave Beth her phone number. "If there's anything we can ever do to help, please let us know."

Beth then called Bob's daughter. Lisa Thomas was the manager of the Refuge Rescuers Detective Agency, and was also a private detective. Her younger sister, Julie, was a detective there, and she went with Lisa to the hospital. On the way, she was the one who called Lisa's husband, Mack Thomas. They didn't wait for him to go with them, because when the call came from Beth he was working in the far reaches of the vast, private wildlife refuge that he managed. But he was on his way as soon as he got the call.

When Lisa and Julie got to the hospital, Beth was anxiously waiting for them. "He's in surgery," she told them right away. "Those men beat him up pretty bad. It doesn't look too good. The doctors are worried that his heart might give out."

"Do they know how long it will be before they can tell us what's going on, or how bad he is?"

"No, but you know how doctors are. They don't like saying much until they know for sure."

Julie, who was softly crying now, said, "We can't lose him, Lisa. We just can't. We lost mom way too soon. So we just can't lose dad too."

Lisa shook her head in agreement. She wasn't sure she could deal with another tragedy. She was kidnapped and raped several times when she was sixteen. The men who did it also murdered her mother. And since then a number of other tragedies had occurred in her life. The one thing she knew for sure, whoever did this to her father was going to pay for it. No matter what else happened, she would personally make that happen. One way or the other.

The police made one big mistake when they questioned and accused Beth. They told her the name of the owner of the SUV. At the detective agency, there was a woman named Sue Sartor who was a near genius with computers and doing online research. Lisa called her and put her to work researching that rich insurance man and his entire family. Especially his son, the star quarterback. It wasn't long before Lisa had his photo and history on her cell phone. From that information, she had little doubt about who was driving the SUV when the two women were grabbed.

From then on, they tried to quietly wait for the doctor. It was a long wait and they were all constantly restless while they did. Mack got there before they saw the doctor, so Beth was able to tell him what happened and why.

"So as far as you know," Mack asked, "the police are not going after the man who owns the SUV?"

"From what little I was able to get out of them, it doesn't look like it." Beth frowned, obviously disgusted. "He's one of those important people. I doubt that he was one of the men anyway. From what I could see, they were all pretty young. A couple of them looked more like teenagers than grown men. The son of the SUV owner is still in high school. He's a football player, so the police won't be looking at him as hard as they should."

"I think it's all bullshit," Lisa said. "Odd's are, it was the football player who was driving the damn thing. He's been accused a couple of times of improper behavior with girls, but nothing ever came of it. It's likely the people involved were bought off. And you're right, Beth, if he's a good player, the police aren't likely to go after him near as hard as they should. And this one is their starting quarterback, so they probably won't go after him at all."

"I don't think they will either," Julie said. "Those damn athletes are always getting away with all kinds of shit. No matter what team they play on or where it is. I sure am glad we are detectives. This way, if the cops don't go after the creeps who did what they did, we can."

Two detectives from the local police force joined them then. They didn't look happy. "From what we've learned so far," the lead of the two said to Beth, "things are starting to point to you and your husband as the problem here. According to what we've learned, your husband crashed into the SUV for no good reason."

"That's insane," Beth answered. "Melissa and Jane were being abducted. We had no reason to attack anyone."

"Again, that's not the way it looks. So you are going to have to come with us to the station until we get this all sorted out."

Mack stepped in then. "Are you arresting her?"

"Who the hell are you?"

"Doesn't matter. Answer my question."

"I think you'd best back the hell off, or you will be the one arrested."

"I don't think so. And since you haven't answered my question, I will assume you are not arresting her. In which case, she's going no where or place with you. Not now, not ever. So unless you have something to say about what actually happened, and can tell us you've made some progress in your pursuit of the guilty parties, you can leave now. None of us are in the mood for your chickenshit bullshit."

"You really are looking for trouble," the cop snarled. "And you are in the right place to get it." He grabbed Mack's arm.

Mack pushed his hand away. "Unless you are prepared to have yourself, this city, and your department sued and harassed for the next only god knows how many months, if not years, it would be a good idea for you to back off."

"I've had it with you." He tried to jam his finger into Mack's chest. He never got it that far. Before he even knew what happened, his finger was being twisted to the edge of a significant break.

"I don't like people to do that to me," Mack growled between gritted teeth. "And I've had it with you. It's time for you to get the hell out of here and go do your job. What you're doing right now gives all cops a bad name. And being an ex-cop, that really pisses me off." He twisted the finger a very little bit more.

The cop groaned. He looked at his partner. "Give me a hand here."

His partner didn't move. His eyes stayed on Lisa and Julie. He didn't know why, but something about the way she stood in front of him, told him that it would not only be futile to try to help his partner. It would very foolish. "Sorry," he answered, "I can't right now." He was right. He couldn't. If he tried to get passed Lisa, she would have easily stopped him. She was a fighter, and there were few people anywhere who could have gotten passed her if she didn't want them to.

Mack let go of the finger. "You are leaving now. We will talk to you again when you have some positive news about arresting the actual guilty parties, beginning with your star quarterback. Until then, you will stay the hell away from us."

"What's to stop me from calling for backup?" the cop asked.

"To start, a team of more lawyers than someone with your limited brain could count. After that, it would mean you'd have to take Lisa here on. That would leave you crippled up for quite a while. You've pissed her off. She can get mean when someone as lacking decency as you do, does that."

The cop had been around long enough to know real trouble when he saw it. This was real trouble. It didn't take him but a few moments to realize that continuing his bullying tactics would be a bad choice. He shook his head to show his disgust with the situation, then motioned to his partner, and the two cops walked away. As they did, the number two cop turned his head and gave them a small smile. He was one of the few who wasn't a big sports fan. Especially not football.

Lisa smiled and waved back at him. She then sat down and thought about her father. She knew the odds of his survival were not good. That's when she cried.

CHAPTER 1

The doctor didn't report to them until well into the afternoon. When he did, the news wasn't good. Bob was holding his own, considering the condition of his heart, but he was now in a coma. The doctor wasn't sure for how long. All they could do now was wait.

Since there was nothing anyone could do, Mack and Julie decided to go back home. If needed, they would return the next day. Lisa elected to stay with Beth. At least until Bob was awake or it was nighttime.

Before they left, Mack told Lisa, "I want you to be real careful now. Especially when you go outside. I don't trust anyone involved in this mess. So there's no way of knowing what they might try to do."

"I'll be careful, Mack."

"Good. Now, don't be too late going home tonight."

As it nearly always is the case when a person goes through the trauma they'd just gone through, it was late before Beth and Lisa got at all hungry. When they did, neither one of them could tolerate the thought of hospital food. So Lisa opted to go for some kind of takeout food.

What she didn't know, was that she and Beth were being watched. One of the intensive care nurses was the older sister of a football player. She called her brother as she watched Lisa walk to the elevator that would take her down to the main floor.

The brother was happy to get the call. The word about the trouble makers, who were in one way or the other involved in the earlier interference with the hoped for kidnapping and rape of the two women, was outside of the hospital. Lisa was definitely a person they wanted to deal with in their way.

When he got the call, he and one of his buddies, the star quarterback, Jerry Smith, were out on one of their searches for young women to pickup. Whether the women wanted to be or not. They were only a block away from the hospital, so they easily got there shortly after she was out of the door. They parked their SUV and waited for her, then followed her. They were sure when they tried to take her that it would be an easy task. She was, after all, such a small and delicate woman. Not to mention beautiful. And there was nothing, other than cheers from a grandstand, that was as great as taking what you want from a beautiful, but helpless woman.

These two football players, Jerry Smith and Kelly Morse, did not know anything about Lisa Thomas. She went into self-defense training shortly after she was kidnapped and raped when she was sixteen. She was determined then, that something like that would never happen to her again. So she carried her training much further than only defensive fighting. She was now a real fighter. If there was a tactic that could help her win a fight, she knew it, and wasn't hesitant about using any of them. When she was required to fight, she showed no quarter, and for her, there were no rules. The two males were about to attack and hopefully rape her, simply because she had something to do with Bob and Beth. They had stopped the morning attack on the two innocent women. Something the powerful athletes simply couldn't tolerate.

Given her history as a deputy sheriff and then as a private detective, Lisa was always aware of what was going on around her, so she knew she was being followed. There were only two of them. That meant they didn't concern her a whole lot. She knew what they wanted and what they thought they were going to do to her. They were mistaken. They were going to wish, when she was done with them, that they'd grown up to be decent human beings rather than the trash that they were. This time, any harm done would be done to them.

It order to do that, she wanted more time with them than what she'd get in the main parking lot where her truck was. If she dealt with them there, someone might stop her. So she led them to a very dark corner of the parking lot. She then pretended to stop near one of the cars parked there and let them get close.

Jerry, being the leader of the two, was the first to reach for her. She was smart enough to not let him get his hands on her. Instead, she swung around to greet him with her right arm flying. Her hand reached his face and her nails dug in deep, gouging him above and below his eyes. That held him back as she did a second spin while lifting her left leg. Her foot, covered by a western style, pointed toe boot, connected with Kelly's exposed side, left open by his raised arms.

It was a hard kick and broke two of his ribs. Her spin brought her face to face again with Jerry. She jammed her fist into his solar plexus, doubling him over. She instantly grabbed his hair and brought his face down hard on her rising knee. He went down and she turned again to Kelly who was now holding desperately onto his broken ribs. She could see his pain, but somehow knowing that these two had everything to do with her father lying unconscious in his hospital bed, she showed him no mercy. She kicked him with everything she had, which was a lot, in the groin. He doubled over as he fell to the ground. When he landed, she stomped on his knee. She knew from the crack it made that his football career was over for at least the next season, if not forever.

Jerry was finally trying to get to his feet. Lisa was sure from his looks, that he was one of those males who used his good looks as an excuse to constantly mistreat any girl he ever went out with. So she fixed them some. She slammed the palm of her hand into his nose. It didn't just break. It shattered. She then doubled up her fists and slammed the side of them onto the side of his head. It knocked him to the ground, but didn't totally knock him out. He was going to be in a daze for at least another hour. Lisa then gave him a little knee work. This time the crack it made told her that it would be a very long time before he did any running.

She turned to Kelley, who was the most awake of the two. She held his head by the hair so he was facing her. "It's like this, asshole. You started a war when you beat up my father. What you got tonight is just the beginning of what you'll get if you or any of you chickenshit little bastards ever come anywhere near me or mine again. This time, I'm not going to call any cops. I'm not going to do a damn thing to help you either. I'll be taking your cell phones with me, so if you want any help, you are damn well going to have to crawl to get it."

She found their cell phones then, and calmly walked to her truck. She left to pick up some fried chicken and potato salad. She dropped the cell phones at the reception desk on her way to the elevator in the hospital. She was eating the last piece of chicken when the police arrived. They did not look friendly.

"You are under arrest," the cop who decided to be the leader said to Lisa, after looking the two women over.

"Really?" Lisa then pissed them off by smiling. "And whatever for, am I being arrested?"

"You know damn good and well what for. You assaulted two men out in the parking lot."

Lisa lifted a hand and pointed her thumb at herself. "Me? I? Attacked two men in the parking lot? And how was I supposed to do that? Almost any man is bigger than me. So how the hell could I attack two of them?"

"I don't know. I just know that they swear that you did."

Lisa laughed. "They can swear all they want. You still can't arrest me for it. It's just too obvious that there's no way someone my size could beat up two grownup men. That's what you're talking about aren't you? Grownup men?"

"Well, they're just about grownup men. Senior high school boys actually."

"Really? And how big are they?"

"Well, back when they could still stand up, they were both somewhat over six feet."

"And I assaulted them? Two six foot tall men? I beat them up? Boy, there really isn't anything you won't believe, is there? I don't know what cop school you came from, but it ought to be shut down if you are what it produces."

The cop was now red in the face with his fists tightly clenched. He looked as if he was ready to throw a punch at her. His partner wisely touched his shoulder and nodded his head at the door.

"I think maybe," he said, "that we should have those boys tested for drugs. There just ain't no way a woman her size could have done to the two of them what was done. And she doesn't have a mark on her."

"Yeah, but goddamnit, Jerry was the best quarterback the team's had in more than twenty years. With him there, the title would have been a sure thing this year."

"I know. But arresting the wrong person for what was done to him isn't going to get him back in the game."

Lisa heard enough of their conversation to feel even better about what she did to the two guys who had planned to attack and rape, then probably kill her. It was then though, that she looked down on her blouse. There was just a tell tale sign of blood on her blouse. She realized then that it was the fried chicken that saved her. It was particularly greasy, and mixed in with the blood stains were grease stains. It took a real close look to tell the difference. And stains on her blouse were not the parts of her the cops had been studying. When she thought about that, her smile broadened. It was one thing when men looked. It meant a lot more when they had to pay for it. Those two cops, as well as the two males she left in the parking lot, all paid for it this time.

CHAPTER 2

Lisa was so concerned about Beth, and how she was dealing with all that had happened, that she forgot to pay any attention to the time. It was near ten-thirty when Mack called her. He was concerned that she hadn't left for home yet.

"I'm sorry, Mack," she told him. "I know I should have called you or left for home or something by now. But I'm kind of concerned about Beth, so I just forgot to pay any attention to anything else."

"It's okay, Lisa. I understand. But you know me. I always worry when things like this happen and I don't know for sure what's going on. Are you coming home tonight? If not, that's okay. If you are though, I think it'd be best if you do it soon. I hate thinking about you out on the highway alone so late at night, even if you are fighter enough to beat the shit out of two full grown football players."

"How the hell did you find out about that?"

"Dale told me. After the police talked to you about it, they called him to see if he knew anything about you. Since I told him what is going on, he played ignorant for them. For now, you should be okay with them. So are you coming home or not?"

"I'm coming home. Other than keep Beth company, there's nothing I can do here. Not as long as Dad is still in a coma anyway. I'll be leaving shortly."

"Good. That's real good, Lisa. Just remember to be real careful. And more than that, remember how much I love you."

"I love you too, Mack."

Lisa talked to Beth for a few minutes then, voicing her concern about leaving her alone for the night.

"I'll be fine," Beth told her. "It's late now, and I'm tired enough, so I should be able to get some sleep on the cot the nurses set up for me. And Mack's right. You should get home before it gets too late. Given the world we live in now, a woman alone out on the highway late at night is not a good idea. Not even for a woman with your talents."

Lisa smiled at her last comment, then they made their goodbyes.

She didn't know why, but Lisa suddenly got a crawling feeling of something wrong as soon as she stepped from the elevator onto the main floor of the hospital. Rather than leave the building right away, she looked out the glass doors at the main entrance. The SUV parked close by told her everything she needed to know.

Two rather large males, who looked to be somewhere near the age of eighteen, stood next to it. The doors of the vehicle were open, so she could see four more males near the same age sitting inside it.

In a perverted sort of way, she was a little bit proud of herself. She had made them afraid of her enough so they thought they needed six of them to get to her. At the same time, she was smart enough to not even consider taking on all of them together. Maybe as many as three of them. But not six. That was just too many.

Under any other circumstances, she would have called the police and at least asked for an escort to her pickup. Not here. She had no doubt that they were highly unlikely to have any inclination to protect her from their precious athletes. A woman being beaten and raped wasn't near as serious as the high school team losing a football game.

That left her to find her own way out. She knew that she had no chance to make it to her truck before they caught her if she tried to run for it. All the other exits would leave her in the open even farther than the main entrance. That left one chance. Get them to chase her, so they were all behind her. Football players or not, she was confident she could run fast enough to reach the safety of her pickup before they caught up with her, just as long as all six of them were behind her.

But if they did catch her, what then? She sighed. The hell with it. She'd use death blows on at least two of them, then do as much damage as she could before it was over. However it ended, they would all regret what they did. And even if she didn't manage to do that much damage on her own, someday, somehow, Mack eventually would.

Having made her decision, Lisa opened one of the main doors. She held it open and as soon as they saw her, she lifted her middle finger and gave them a big smile.

Knowing that now timing was everything, she didn't wait for their response. She immediately headed for an emergency exit only.

Alarms went off as she slammed it open and rushed through. The sudden wailing of the sirens going off brought the six mighty males chasing her to a brief halt. It proved to be just enough for her to reach her pickup and get in it and lock it before they reached her.

She only had two blocks to go, from the hospital parking lot to the entrance of the freeway. She was doing an easy ninety miles an hour in a couple of minutes. It was a speed she could continue driving with far more safety than most people. Years before, when she was a deputy sheriff, she had used her own pickup as the official vehicle she drove while on duty. It had been equipped with everything a deputy sheriff needed. All that equipment was still part of it. So she turned on her lights and siren, then used her radio to contact the Clayborne County Sheriff's Department.

The dispatcher knew Lisa well, and after Lisa explained what was happening, she assured her that there would be a special interception waiting for the SUV now running tight on her tail.

Lisa then called Mack and told him what was happening. His answer was exactly what she expected. "I'm on my way."

The driver of the SUV decided then that he was going to get around her and force her to pull over. He was sure that he could easily out drive her. She couldn't possibly stand a chance against his superior athletic ability, which he was sure way beyond any doubt at all, was way better than hers.

Lisa wasn't at all intimidated by his move. As a deputy sheriff, she received many hours of driver's training, just for situations like this one. She thought about her options. She knew she could out maneuver him in any way she wanted to, up to and including pushing the six men/boys in the SUV into a deadly crash. At ninety miles an hour, if a serious crash didn't leave them dead, they would be at least fairly well messed up.

She decided instead, to just give the driver a few lessons. At will, she several times put them in near crash positions, just letting up at the last second. By the time they crossed the county line into Clayborne county, the contest was over and the SUV was permanently behind her.

As it was prearranged over the radio, about five miles south of Kingsburg, where the sheriff's office was located, three sheriff's cars appeared with their lights flashing and sirens wailing. The SUV had no choice but to pull over. Lisa parked in front of the lead patrol car.

She stood close as the six males, who were previously so intent on doing her some kind of harm, climbed out of their SUV. They were forced to lean against it with their legs spread wide as they were not too gently searched. They were next told to lay down on the ground with their hands behind them and were then handcuffed.

A thorough search of the SUV was made. Inside they found marijuana in quantities far greater than what was legal for personal use. There were also two open bottles of alcoholic beverages. One was whisky, the other vodka. That meant they would be charging the six with crimes that went beyond what they'd attempted to do to Lisa.

Mack got there then. He was steaming angry. He walked up to the closest man on the ground, grabbed his hair and pulled his head up, snapping his neck enough to be very painful.

"That was my wife you assholes were after. I don't take this kind of shit lightly. So you'd best remember, when all of this is said and done, I will be coming for you." He dropped the head. He looked at sheriff Dale Magee. "Sorry about that, Dale, but I had to do something."

"I understand," Dale said. "I'm just glad you didn't kill him. I'd hate to have to lock up my best friend."

"I have to admit, I was tempted."

The six were taken to the sheriff's office and locked up. They all demanded to be allowed to make a phone call immediately. Dale didn't give into their demands. First, he made sure all the proper paper work was completed. Since there were six of them, and they only did it one man at a time, it took most of the night. During that time, none of them were offered anything to eat or drink.

Mack and Lisa went along so they could watch the six locked up. Lisa especially wanted to be there as their cell doors were closed and locked. It gave her a sense of justice to see it, after barely escaping the fate that would have awaited her if they'd caught her.

They, on the other hand, couldn't believe what was happening to them. Always in the past they'd been able to do what they wanted when they wanted. Which was, from their point of view, the way it should be. They were special people and deserved everything they ever got. How could anyone consider anything more important than winning at sports. It was everything. And they were among the chosen few who could do that. But now here they were, locked up in a place where people actually believed that a mere woman like Lisa Thomas was more important than they were. Considering any woman better or even equal to a man was simply wrong. A woman, who was just a country girl, being considered better than six fine athletes was completely insane. Beautiful or not, she was only valuable as a body to satisfy their urges. Whatever they might be.

Someday, somehow, the idea that anyone could be as important as they were would have to be changed in this place. As far as they were concerned, Lisa was right about one thing and one thing only. It was when she told their leader, Jerry Smith, the star quarterback, that they were in a war now. Other than that there was no way she was right about anything. All six of them agreed, this was now all out war. Once they were free again, it would be all the athletes they could bring into their group, along with fans young and old alike, who would in one way or another be going after all those Andersons and Thomases and members of this county's sheriff's department. Ultimately, there was no way they could compete with the tough guys who played football. Not even with those who played other sports. These people were only a bunch of country hicks who would never be able to hold up against the strength and power of well trained athletes.

CHAPTER 3

Mack and Lisa's home was next to a meadow that was part of a four hundred acre ranch/farm. When Mack bought it, he planned on raising beef cattle on it with his uncle Roy and Roy's wife Wanda. Mack's father, Ben, also raised forty acres of vegetables there. Over time, their life's experiences had changed it considerably. Ben still raised his vegetables, but the cattle were gone.

Mack and Lisa were deputy sheriffs when it started, but had moved on to start a private detective agency called Refuge Rescuers. Mack originally managed it, but he left it and took over the management of a private wildlife refuge. Lisa now managed the agancy. The land itself now held several homes, along with the offices for Refuge Rescuers. Nearly everyone connected with the agency lived in a home on the four hundred acres.

Years earlier, Mack and Ben started everyday eating breakfast together. That activity had since grown into a tradition which included everyone who was part of the agency or the wildlife refuge. It served them as not only the chance to eat a great breakfast that Ben and his wife, Theresa, cooked, but also as a meeting place where they could all keep each other informed of what was going on in their worlds. Two worlds that were vastly different, yet tightly woven together.

This morning it afforded Mack, Lisa, and Julie the opportunity to tell everyone what happened to Bob and Beth, and what Lisa did to the football players. Everyone there knew Lisa, so it didn't come as any surprise that she disabled two football players intent on raping her. They agreed too, that leading the six who were after her into a trap was a wise thing to do. The more men like them in a hospital bed or a jail cell, the better.

The person who Mack considered as his partner in the wildlife refuge, but who thought of herself as his assistant, Shanty Lucas, asked him the first question. "Will you be working with Lisa, helping Bob and Beth?"

"I'll be going with her today, when she goes to the sheriff's office to file the complaints against the ones who were locked up last night. After that, we'll just have to wait and see. It'll all depend more on what those people do than anything else."

"Okay, Mack. I'm not complaining. You need to do what you need to do. And family always comes first. I just wanted some idea of what you'd be doing so I can plan accordingly. You know I don't like to make any important decisions about anything in the refuge without you knowing what they are."

"I know, but I trust you to always do the right thing. Not to mention, if it weren't for you, there wouldn't be so many decisions to make right now."

Shanty was a billionaire several times over, and she had spent a huge amount of money to buy land to expand the refuge. She owned a large percentage of a gun manufacturing corporation that was among the largest in the world. She'd given up the management of it so she could work with Mack to bring the refuge to what it had originally been when the federal government set it up back in the sixties. She did it not only for the refuge itself. She also did it to be as close to Mack as she could. She loved him, and it was the only way she could be a large part of his life. She also loved and respected Lisa, so her relationship with Mack going in any other direction than what it was already in, was out of the question. Shanty worked every day with Mack. Lisa was the one who got to live and sleep with him.

The wildlife refuge was now a private enterprise that existed on what money she and Mack invested, and from donations from those knowing people who understood how important places like it were. Not only for animal and plants. They were something much needed for the human spirit as well. Even those who didn't at all appreciate it.

For Mack, just working in the refuge every day was part of a dream he'd had since he was a kid living next to it. He spent as many hours in it while he was growing up as was possible, and loved everything about it. Now, to not only be working in it, but to be able to be part of restoring it, took him beyond his wildest dreams. He was rich because of an inheritance, but what he was doing now meant far more to him than any amount of money ever could. For him, money could easily become a burden he neither needed nor wanted.

He had loved being a deputy sheriff, and then a private detective, but both occupations tended to take him into too many violent situations. Leaving them, to do what he was doing in and for the refuge was easy. The trouble was, he was never able to entirely escape the previous work. Far more than he wanted, he was asked to assist the agency with difficult cases. And this time it was family who were the ones who were the difficult case. That left no doubt that he would be involved. Especially given the fact that the most important person in the world to him, his wife, Lisa, was so directly a major part of it.

Shanty understood and appreciated all that, so she asked, "What is that I can do, Mack? If nothing else, we need to be sure everyone who is part of what happened yesterday is protected."

"You're right about that. Especially any of us who have to be at or near the hospital. I think to start with, we should get around the clock protection for Beth and Bob as long as they are there, or if Bob needs to go into a rehabilitation clinic after he's released from the hospital."

"I can take care of that," Shanty offered. "There'll be bodyguards outside of Bob's room within a couple of hours. They'll be there around the clock. For about ten hours during the day, there will someone to go with Beth for anything she needs to do or any place she needs to go."

"That's great, Shanty. Just be damn sure you have them send me the bill."

"Don't be ridiculous, Mack. I own the company who will be providing the service. It stops there. I'm part of all of you now, so you have to let me do what little to help I can do when I can do it."

"I know, but you've given all of us so much already."

"Oh hell, Mack, it's nothing important. It's just money. All the rest that we have, that we share, is a hell of a lot more important than money."

Larry Jameson, who was one of Refuge Rescuers's detectives spoke up then. But he did it with a smile. "That's easy to say, Shanty, when you've always had it. For those of us who haven't always had enough, it can sometime seem important." Larry was a recluse living up in the wilds of Canada for several years, so he was well aware of what it was like to live with little or no money.

"I know that, just as I know that even if it's easy for me to say it's only money, it's still true. It's only money. Since I've been here working and living with all of you, I've learned that lesson better than any of the others you have all taught me. I now live in a house smaller by far than anything else in my whole life. I eat food I cook myself. Food mostly grown by all of you. It's been months since I spent anything on clothes, and the last time I did, it was for work clothes for my days in the refuge. There's any number of other things I haven't done that used to be a regular part of my life that all cost money. Without all that shit, I've been happier than I ever was before. Life here, living it the way all of you do is the best thing that could ever have happened to me. So yes, Larry, it's only goddamn money. Something that I no longer give one good rat's ass about. Not unless, anyway, I can use it to help someone else. Especially one of you."

"I'm sorry, Shanty, if you think I was putting you down or something. That's not at all what I meant. I only meant that just because the stuff is so often used the wrong way, doesn't make it useless. It can be both good and evil. The thing is, the way you and Mack use it, it is so often a good thing. So it's not an it's only money thing. Coming from you guys, it's a good thing. What you're doing in and with the refuge alone is enough to prove that point."

Mack chuckled at their comments, even though he knew they were both right. But he couldn't let them go by without a comment of his own. "You're both right," he said, a broad grin on his face, "but I have to say, having too much of it can often be an extremely large pain in the ass."

Those words were so much of what and who Mack Thomas was, that they brought affirmative nods from everyone at that extra large breakfast table.

As soon as the meal was done, Mack and Lisa left for Kingsburg and the sheriff's office. The first of the parents arrived shortly after they did. As was all too often the case, they were completely irate over the fact that their precious little one (he was six feet two inches tall and weighed in at two hundred fifty pounds of muscle) had been arrested and held in a regular jail cell. They demanded his immediate release.

"You'll have to wait until the judge sets the bail," Sheriff Dale Magee explained, "at which time you will be required to pay it in cash. We don't take checks or credit cards. That is, of course, providing the judge grants bail. Given how serious the charges agains him are, there's a possibility he won't."

"Serious charges?" the father screamed. "That's total nonsense. He didn't do anything. He was just riding in the backseat of someone else's car."

"The driver of that car was doing everything he could to run another vehicle off the road. That would have likely caused a serious accident. It is also a fact that your son, along with five other individuals, attempted to abduct a lone female from the hospital. Given the past history of all six of the males involved in the attempted abduction, we are charging them with the intent to kidnap and rape the woman involved. We might even charge all of them with attempted murder, based on what they did on the highway. And even if the murder charge doesn't take, there were drugs and two open bottles in the car. He will be held accountable for that."

The father looked around the office. His eyes stopped on Lisa, who was quietly sitting next to Mack. She was the only female there who was not wearing a uniform. He pointed at her.

"Is she the goddamn little whore who's causing all this. It's easy to see that she's nothing but a tramp. There's no way I'm going to let a two-bit sheriff like you put her ahead of my son. Either you release him now, or you will regret it big time."

"Really? And how am I going to do that?"

"Simple. You are going to go down. If I can't get it done through the law, there's a lot of other ways to do it. Where I come from, we have ways to deal with smalltime little nothings like you."

"So what are you going to do. Have someone beat me up or something."

"Damn right. Although in your case, I don't think I'll have them stop with a beating. Not with with the little whore over there either."

That was all Mack was about to listen to. He started to move toward the irate father. Before he could get to him, Dale turned him around and cuffed the man. It only took the motion of his finger to bring two deputies, who heard every word the father said, over to him.

"Lock him up," Dale told him. "I'll decided on the charges later." He turned to the wife of the irate father. "You might as well go home now. It'll be at least a day or two before that man will be getting out of here. There's no way that we'll be able to get the paperwork done in time for the hearing today. And he will have to post bail before he gets out of here."

"I won't be leaving this crummy little town without my son and my husband," she growled. "And after I do, you will definitely be sorry you ever did this to us."

"Are you threatening me too?" Dale asked.

"No. I'm not going to let you lock me up too. But I am going to wait here until my husband is released."

"That's fine with me, but the only accommodations we have are the chairs in the office here. Unless you want to sleep in a jail cell. The problem there is the fact that we are limited in the amount of space we have. So if you do decide to sleep in one of the cells, you'll have to share it with whoever already occupies it. And right now, everyone who is locked up is a male. You will be the only female there."

"What do you expect me to do then?"

"Whether your son gets released or not, going home would be a good idea."

"I can't do that. I can't just leave my husband here."

"Why not?" Dale asked. "I think that life there would be a lot more pleasant than normal without him around."

She answered with a heavy sigh, then said, "That's not a very nice thing to say."

"Probably not, but when it comes to people like your husband, it is often near impossible to find anything nice."

She shook her head. "Is there a motel in town?"

Dale gave her directions to three of them that were within a reasonable distance, then reminded her of the time of the hearing.

She then gave Dale a sad, somewhat distant look. "It's kind of too bad I'm not about ten years younger. If I were then maybe I could talk you into showing me where one of those places is." A single tear rolled down her cheek as she turned and left the office.

Dale watched her go, wondering once again why there were so many people who seemingly had it all, actually had nothing that really mattered. It made him sad, so to lift his spirits he turned to Mack and Lisa and gave them the best smile he could manage. They returned it.

Knowing he was going to have to go through more of the same crap, Mack and Lisa couldn't help but feel bad for him. Since though, there was nothing they could do to help, they left him.

Mack wanted to go back to work in the refuge, but because of his concern for Lisa, he drove her to the hospital. She was grateful for his company, even though Beth was still there and Julie had gotten there earlier.

Once there, while she watched her father struggle so hard to live, having Mack next to her, especially with him holding her hand, gave her a kind of comfort and reassurance to face it she never would have had without him.

Julie and Beth watched the two of them. Even with all their other concerns, both of those two woman found themselves wishing it was their hand he would be holding.

CHAPTER 4

It didn't take long before time started to drag. Chairs in any hospital are at best manageable. In this hospital, they were not exactly the best. So along with the boredom from the inability to do anything about the problem that brought them there, they were forced to endure the discomfort of ill-fitting chairs.

Conversation quickly wore down. The concern for Bob was the overriding thought on their minds, and they quickly expressed them in every way possible. Mack, Lisa, and Beth gradually settled into reading a book on their cell phones. For Mack, it was one of the few things he considered them good for. Julie, on the other hand, kept herself busy texting with friends.

They somehow managed to cope with the situation into the afternoon. Mack was the first of them to notice his hunger. He attempted to ignore it for a while, but when his stomach growled at him with a definite complaint he decided it was time to mention it.

"Is anyone else hungry?" he asked. "Because I am more than ready to get something to eat."

"I am," Lisa responded right away.

Beth hesitated a moment. The look on her face said she would feel guilty about doing anything more than wait for Bob to wake up. She especially didn't think she should go anywhere before he did. "I don't think I want to eat right now," she finally answered.

Julie was in the middle of a text message when Mack mentioned his hunger, and she finished it before she acknowledged his question. "I'm not super hungry or anything," she answered. "But I guess I could eat."

Lisa was the one who answered Beth. "You have to eat," she told her. "So I think you should go with Julie and Mack. I'll stay here, so you don't have to feel bad about leaving Dad here alone."

"I think it would be a damn good idea for you to get out of this hospital for a while too," Mack told her. "No matter what happens, we won't be gone that long. There's a long line of fast food joints a couple of blocks from here, so we can make a quick meal out of it. And while we're gone, there is a guard on duty outside his room now."

"I know. I'll still feel awful guilty if I got too far away from him. I think you guys should go out and eat. You can bring me some takeout when you come back."

"We could do that, Beth," Lisa said. "But the truth is, it would be a lot better if you were to come along with us. You need to get out of here for a while. Otherwise, it could leave you crazy. When dad gets out of here, he'll need you to not be crazy." The look she gave Beth then had nothing but love and concern in it. Beth finally relented, and they stood to go.

Mack told the guard sitting next to the door to Bob's room, "We're going to grab something to eat. While we're gone, no one other than medical people goes in the room. No matter who they say they are."

"I know. I'll keep a close eye on things."

"Good. Can we bring you back something to eat?"

"Sure. And I don't much care what. Just bring something from wherever you go. Anything will be better than what I normally eat on this kind of duty."

"We will bring you something then," Mack promised.

Before they got out of the waiting room, a young man who was sitting on the far side of the room the whole time approached them. "I'm the man who's been sent here to guard Beth. So as much as I hate to intrude on you, I will have to go along with you. If you are going out to eat, I will sit away from you so you can have your privacy. But I do have to be where I can see her. Someone was concerned enough about her safety to hire me to keep her safe, so that's what I have to do."

"I understand," Mack answered. "You can follow us when we leave. When we do stop somewhere, you'll be more than welcome to join us while we eat. There's no damn sense in your going hungry."

"Well, thanks for the offer, but I pretty much don't want to interfere with anything you might want to do."

Mack smiled. "It wasn't an offer. It was an invitation. We've all been there at one time or another, so we aren't about to let you go hungry while you sit alone while we eat. While you're at our table, we can all keep on the lookout for trouble. There's no reason for you to go hungry."

"Well, I guess I can do that if it's okay with all of these ladies."

Julie answered first. "It's plenty okay with me," she said, her face coloring slightly. Lisa and Beth just nodded their agreement.

"I think though," the young guard said, "I'd prefer it if all of you would ride with me. I'm driving a SUV big enough for all of us to ride comfortable. And that way there's no chance for us to get split up."

"You know, don't you," Lisa told him, "that we are all perfectly capable of taking care of ourselves."

He answered her with the best smile he could put together. "I do. I was thoroughly briefed before I was sent here. That's not the point though. I'm here to protect Beth, regardless of anything else. So to the best of my ability, that's exactly what I'm going to do."

Since she was the center of the conversation, Beth voiced her opinion. "We'll ride with you. There's just no point in any of us doing anything to interfere with you doing your job. Besides, if we do run into any trouble, having us all together will be a better defense than having us split up would be."

No one argued that decision. Not even Lisa. She made her point and was satisfied with it.

The young guard finally introduced himself. "I'm Lenard, by the way. Lenard Shultz." He quickly shook everyone's hand. "And my nickname is not Lennie. Lenard works fine. I don't care much for Lennie."

Lisa couldn't help herself. "I hate the name, Lennie," she said, "So you'll never hear me call you that."

Lenard was somewhat startled by the tone of Lisa's voice when she answered him. Mack explained. "It's a long story and was the worst kind of experience she could have ever had. Someday, maybe we'll explain it all to you."

Lenard nodded his head, then led them to his car. Everyone was surprised when Julie claimed the passenger seat in the front. Mack frowned a bit about having to ride in the back seat, but Lisa and Beth got a chuckle out of Julie's antics. She was not even making the slightest attempt to hide the fact that she was interested in the young guard, Lenard Shultz.

As they drove along the takeout food row, Mack, who was next to the window on the right side, spotted a sign for an old-fashioned Chinese takeout place. It didn't take any argument to get everyone to agree that it was the place to go. The sign for it was out near the road they were on, but the restaurant was located in an alley, about a half block from the road they were on. When they parked, they were left with the equivalent of nearly a city block to walk. Inside, there were only a few small tables. None of them were occupied.

After asking if it was okay, they pushed a couple of them together so all five of them could sit together. Julie made sure she got one of the chairs next to Lenard. He tried not to notice, but failed completely at that exorcise. They were given menus, and Mack more than any of them was delighted to see that they served all of the Chinese type food that had once been commonly available, but that had now mostly disappeared from the fast food scene.

When it came to order, they all ordered one kind of dish or another. Mack stayed with the things he'd eaten in his youth. Chow mien, fried rice, eggs foo young, and a couple of egg rolls. It had been years since he'd eaten that particular kind of food, and he relished every bite of it. Everyone else thought their food was pretty good, but none of them got quite the same kind of pleasure out of the meal Mack did. Julie didn't notice either way. Her attention was focussed on something else.

When the meal was done, the women decided on what to bring the guard still at the door of Bob's hospital room. While they waited for that takeout food order to be brought to their table, a couple come in and studied their faces for a moment as they stood by the counter where they ordered takeout. The woman then made a call on her cell phone. She spoke so softly into it that no one could hear what she said, but she shook her head yes quite vigorously while she talked.

Lisa, who for reasons even she wasn't sure of, started watching the woman. Something unexpectedly happened to her then. Her gut tightened up and she felt as though something was wrong. Something that was very wrong. She took Mack's hand and squeezed it hard. He knew the instant he felt it that she was reacting to something.

"I got it," he said, very softly. "Trouble somewhere."

Lenard, being the professional that he was, right away picked up on the look on their faces. He held up his hand slightly, telling them to stay seated, but didn't say anything until the couple was given their takeout order and left. "What is it?" he asked then.

Lisa answered. "Trouble, maybe. I can't be sure, but I think that couple who was just in here knew who we are. That phone call she made was too quiet. There was something about them that bothered me. I don't know what exactly, but there was definitely something wrong."

"It's not likely that anyone will do anything now. It's broad daylight and this place is too close to a busy street. What do you think anyone is going to try to do?"

"It could be anything," she explained. "There's a lot of people around here who hate us. Me in particular. I'm the bitch who's out of line for not allowing a couple of football players to rape and perhaps murder me. After all, they win football games. I'm just a somewhat useless female."

"But it's still light outside. If they try anything now, people will see them. Why would anyone try anything now, when they likely will end up arrested for it."

"Because they won't be. It seems as though a good percentage of the police force here is made up of football fans. They'll be slow coming and they'll do nothing to help us when they get here. We might even be the ones they arrest."

"Well, we can't have that, now can we?" He smiled. "You guys all stay here for a bit. I'm going to go outside and check on what's going on."

Mack stood up. "I should go with you. It's not right that you should go out there alone. It is our fight."

"It's mine now too. I know enough about you, Mack, to know that you understand that. They aren't going to do anything to me. I'll be fine out there. I just want to defuse this situation before the five of us are forced to hurt anyone. So please, give me a few minutes."

Lenard was outside for nearly fifteen minutes. The four who were left inside could not see nor hear anything while he was gone. His expression was one of satisfaction when he returned.

"It'll only about twenty or thirty minutes to wait. Then we'll get out of here. There won't be any trouble when we do. That's gone for now. But all of you have to be damn careful in the future. There does appear to be quite a few people around here who think a jackass quarterback is about the most valuable thing the human race can produce."

Julie put her hand on his shoulder then, and gave him a smile that on her beautiful face said more than any words could. "I think," she said to him, and to him alone, "people who guard lives are worth a hell of a lot more than any kind of football player alive. Now are we going to quit fooling around with this and are you going to ask me out or what?"

CHAPTER 5

Lenard didn't tell them what it was he did to gain them safe passage through the crowd waiting outside the Chinese restaurant when they left it. But there were several local police officers there to control the situation. Along with them, three men in dark blue suits walked with them to Lenard's SUV. Mack knew right away, from the fit of their clothes, that they were heavily armed.

The hospital entrance was clear when they got back there, and there were no further incidents that day. Mack, Lisa and Julie stayed through the afternoon. When they decided it was time to go home, Beth opted to stay another night.

They made their goodbyes then, but needed to wait a few extra minutes for Julie. She had to say a special goodbye in a quiet corner of the waiting area. She carrying a happy face when they left the hospital.

The ride home was quiet, and the only thing Julie had to say the whole time, was a goodnight when they dropped her off.

"I think," Lisa said after they did, "my little sister has grown up."

"There's no doubt about it," Mack agreed. "But grown up or not, we are going to have Sue check out Lenard Schultz. With things the way they are now, we can't be too careful."

"I can't argue with you on that, Mack. My gut feeling though, is that Lenard is a lot more than a bodyguard. It took more than a few words to accomplish what he did at the restaurant today. He's got to be connected to something to have the power to get those local cops to protect us instead of trying to hang us for some made up crime or another."

"I think so too. Especially since Shanty was the one who hired him. There's something about having billions of dollars that puts a person in a different position than us normal folks."

"That's true, Mack. Still, we can't really get too negative about it. We are a long way from being billionaires, yet when it comes to money we have a hell of a lot less to worry about than most folks do. And I don't think you could call us all that normal either."

"I know. And I doubt I'll ever stop feeling somewhat guilty about the money, nor will I ever feel what one could call normal. Even when I'm working in the refuge, what I'm doing is off the beaten path."

"I know you won't ever feel good about having the money. The thing is though, you shouldn't feel bad. Most of it you've had has gone for something beyond our basic needs. You've helped a lot of people who have needed it."

"That might be true, Lisa. Still, there are a lot of days I pretty much would like to be rid of all of it. It can weigh a person down."

"When you feel that way, you have to be thinking about Shanty too. We have a few millions. She's saddled with several billions. It's hard to imagine how difficult it must be to constantly carry around that kind of weight day after day."

"It is. The trouble is, with all my complaints about carrying burdens, I have to admit that I have it awful good. Most of my days are spent fulfilling a lifelong dream. Working in the refuge. Coming home every night to the most beautiful woman in the world. Someone I love more that anything. Even life itself."

Lisa smiled at his words and moved close enough to wrap her arms around him. "Those feelings go both ways, Mack Thomas. And because they do, I think that the first thing you're going to have to do is wash my back while I take a shower. I need to get rid of the feel of the hospital. After you dry me off all over, we will probably be forced to lay down in our king size bed for a while. We can always get dressed and eat supper later. Much later maybe."

Mack did the best he could to follow her instructions. Without planning it, they fell asleep shortly after he finished with all of the things she wanted done.

They woke a couple of hours later to a ringing phone. It was Beth. "He's awake," she said. "Bob's awake now. His head is much clearer than what the doctor's expected. They said they think he'll even be able to leave the hospital in a day or two. He'll have to go into a rehabilitation clinic for a while, but there's one of them in Kingsburg."

Lisa couldn't answer her. The relief she felt from learning that her father was going to live was too strong. She was crying. Mack finished the conversation with Beth, then held Lisa until the tears stopped and she was breathing normal again.

For the next two days Mack and Lisa visited Bob at the hospital, then at the rehabilitation center in Kingsburg. Once he was settled in there, Mack went back to work in the wildlife refuge. Shanty was more than delighted to have him back, she was ecstatic about it.

"I can't begin to tell you, Mack," she said, "how much I've missed you being here. I love what we're doing to this place. I truly do. Watching this land return to what it once was is awesome. Good as that is, it's only great when I'm sharing those feelings with you."

"I feel the same way about sharing all this with you, Shanty. I never forget that most of what we're getting done is because of you. What you're doing here is one of the best things anyone has ever done anywhere. And you're doing it for so little reward."

"No, I'm not. I'm getting more from this than anything I've ever done. Just working with you everyday is worth everything I've ever had. There's only one other thing on this earth I want."

Mack looked in her eyes. He could see the longing there. Part of him wished he could sooth it. At the same time he knew it wasn't going to happen. He was sure that if he ever gave into Shanty, Lisa would be deeply hurt by it. She'd had enough hurt in her life. She didn't need him to add to it.

Even with all that though, Mack managed to give Shanty enough of a hug and kiss to reassure her of how much he cared for her. It wasn't the same love he had for Lisa. That was something that could never be duplicated. It did however, go far beyond just a simple friendship or working relationship.

"You know don't you, Mack, that as much as what you just did means to me, it'll never be what I really want." She took a deep breath, then laughed a little. "But I guess I'm going to have to stay hot and bothered. What you have with Lisa is too important for us to be any kind of relationship than what we have now."

Mack hesitated for a moment, looking for some kind of positive answer to give her when a distinctive but familiar sound came from a patch of nearby brush.

"I've been wondering how long it would be before she joined us," Shanty said. "She's not been happy the days you've been gone." Shanty laughed hard. "It appears that you've got more than just us human females wanting your attention."

Mack looked up and waved at the most unusual friend he'd ever had. She was a full grown brown bear. She weighed in at just over two hundred and fifty pounds, and when she stood upright she was somewhat over six feet tall.

She was a regular visitor to the refuge, and always looked for Mack while she was there. She had even come to his rescue a few times. That wasn't what she was there for on this day. As soon as she had his attention, she stood up and waved her front paws at him, as if she was scolding him for being absent on her last few visits.

When she dropped down on all four paws again, she walked up to him, pushed her nose into his stomach, then turned around and walked slowly back into the brush.

"That's something else," Shanty said. "It's pretty damn close to unbelievable. If she was some kind of captive bear, it might be possible. She's wild, and still she adopted you. I doubt there's many humans anywhere who could have the kind of effect on wild animals that you do, Mack."

"I don't know what it is either," he answered. "All I've ever done for her is leave her the hell alone. It's her who has done for me."

"Yes, and you make damn sure that everyone else treats her right too. Somehow she knows that, and she's made you her person. Watching you and her is a part of what makes my working here every day such a pure pleasure. I just hope she never gets jealous of our relationship. If she did, I think I could be in big trouble."

"That's possible I guess, so we'll have to watch for any signs of that. The thing I want you to remember, Shanty. No matter what, you are on my short list of what really matters to me and to life in general. I for sure would never want you to be hurt in any way. If there ever comes a time that there's a problem between you and her, I'll be taking your side."

"Hell, I know that, Mack. I just find it fascinating, the way you attract so damn many females. And now, they don't even have to be human."

Mack couldn't come up with a good answer for her, so he stayed quiet. It was time for them to get to work anyway. There was always a lot of work to be done when there was a wildlife refuge the process of being restored.

CHAPTER 6

When Sue completed her research on Lenard Shultz, she asked Lisa to come to her office. "I have some interesting things to tell you about Julie's new friend."

Julie was waiting with Sue when Lisa joined them. She wasn't particularly happy about Sue checking up on Lenard, but she wasn't upset about it either. She knew, given her position in the Refuge Rescuers agency, and even more, the fact she was Lisa's sister, that he would be thoroughly checked out.

"The main thing is, he's a US Marshal. Given his age, that's a pretty high rank. Most people his age would still be a Deputy Marshal. He's a college graduate. He comes from a mostly blue collar working family. He has one aunt who is a doctor. She's the only one I've found who you would call a professional. His record is clean. I couldn't even find a traffic ticket. He was engaged for about six months, but that relationship was broken off a year ago. Her name was Shiela James. She has a record of drug use. It's probably the cause of the split-up with Lenard."

"Do you think maybe now," Julie asked, "that it might be okay if I go out with him?"

"I have never said it wasn't," Lisa answered. "You aren't the only reason we wanted him checked out. When he got that mob at the restaurant backed off the way he did, we knew he had to be more than just a bodyguard. The fact that he's working so close to Beth has a lot to do with it too. So there's no reason for you to be upset about us checking on him."

"I'm not upset. I would though, like to have any relationship I might possibly have with him private."

"As much as possible, you will have it."

"Are you concerned about him and Beth or something?"

"Only for her safety. I'm sure he's only there to look out for her. We just want to be sure there's nothing else that could in any way harm her. We need to keep an eye on Dad too. He's a lot safer now, then he was in the hospital, but given the kind of people who put him there we do need to be careful."

"Okay, Lisa. Just give me all the privacy you can, will you please. I would like to have at least a part of a life that's my own."

It took an effort for Lisa to hide her smile. "We will do our best to do that," she agreed, biting her tongue to keep herself from telling her sister that she should be careful when she was with a man. "But you have always known that being part of this agency will always take some of that away."

Lisa went back to her office and called Mack. She knew he'd be anxious to learn about Lenard. Having the information about him right away meant he wouldn't need to wait any longer before he could ask Shanty about him.

She wasn't surprised when Mack did. "He agreed to be Beth's guard as a personal favor to me. His father and I worked together when my company stopped making assault rifles. As far as anyone knows, he's a foreman at the factory. He actually holds a much higher position, all be it still unofficial. That's left him in a better position to negotiate with the employees who were decidedly unhappy about the transition from making guns to quality cooking utensils."

"How did Lenard mange to take on the job while he's still a US Marshal?"

"Money, Mack. I don't always need to spend it, for it to still have a lot of influence in the right places. And the truth is, he is still on the job. It's just in a little different capacity than normal."

"That must be the reason he had so much influence on those cops who controlled the mob outside the restaurant. They were forced to respect his authority?"

"That's pretty much it, yes."

"Is there a reason why you didn't tell me up front who he really is?"

"Only the dumbest reason there is. It didn't occur to me that it mattered. All that seemed to matter was that Beth was protected."

Mack couldn't help but chuckle at her answer. It was the last reason he expected her to give, but the one that made the most sense. "I guess," he said, "it doesn't look like I have anything to worry about when it comes to Lenard then? Do I?"

"I would say no," Shanty answered, "you really don't."

Under almost any other circumstances, they would have been right. Because there was no direct problem with Lenard to be concerned about. Indirectly, however, there was a serious problem. Shiela James, the woman Lenard was once engaged too, hadn't accepted their breakup. She was still hoping to get back together with him, and one of the things she was doing to make that happen was to follow him as much as she could.

Because she was such an amateur about it, what she was doing was a hit and miss proposition which often left her confused. Her drug use added to it. What she decided, after watching for most of the days Lenard was guarding Beth, was that Beth was Lenard's new love interest. In her addled state, she further decided that she had no choice. She needed to somehow stop the relationship Lenard was having with Beth.

Shiela still had enough of her brain left to figure out who Beth was, and from there, where she lived. She also learned that with Bob in rehabilitation, Beth was spending her nights alone. It was the perfect setup for her to do what she needed to do to remove her from Lenard's life. Shiela convinced herself that once she was gone he would return to her.

It was a dark night when she parked her car out on the road and crept up to Beth's house. She came prepared with a short crowbar, which she used to force open a window. She tried to remain silent as she crawled inside the house. She nearly was, and other than a slight scraping sound she succeeded.

The sound wasn't enough to awaken Beth totally. Instead, it only brought her sleep to a much lighter level. As Shiela approached Beth's bed, she raised her left arm. Her hand had a tight grip on the crowbar, and she was hoping to bring it down on Beth's head.

It was the bad chairs in the hospital waiting room that saved Beth. Because of sitting in them as much as she did, her back muscles were extremely stiff and sore. That tightness radiated down her body and into her legs. When she moved her stiff legs in her sleep, they both cramped hard. She instantly sat up, screaming at the top of her lungs from the pain. It startled Shiela so bad that she dropped the crowbar, turned and ran out of the room. When she reached the window she used to break in, she took a head first dive out it, rather than climb out.

Even in her pain, Beth heard the crowbar drop, then noticed the shadow of Shiela as she scrambled from the bedroom. She was helpless from the leg pain for a couple of minutes, but as soon as the pain subsided enough, she turned on the touch lamp on the table next to her bed. Her cell phone was there next to the lamp, and she called 911. The woman who took the call knew Beth, and like everyone in law enforcement in Clayborne County, knew about what had happened to her and Bob. As soon as she dispatched a sheriff's car to Beth's, she called Dale. He called Mack.

When Mack and Lisa got too Beth's, they found her still badly shaken. The break-in was enough to terrorize her, but the realization that a couple of horrible leg cramps were what saved her life took her over the edge. Everyone had been so concerned and so careful about her safety, and now her life was saved by something so painful no one ever wanted one. And she had two of them. Leg cramps. The whole idea of it freaked her out.

For Mack and Lisa, it was all now a huge concern. They knew they couldn't let Beth stay alone. Whoever it was that broke in to her house and who evidently planned to kill her, was still out there.

After Beth got settled down enough, they brought her home with them. Mack had called Shanty while they were waiting, to let her know that he once again might not be in the refuge until late the next day, if he was there at all. She was up, waiting for them when they got home.

When the subject of where Beth should stay until they could be sure she would be safe going home, Shanty insisted that Beth should stay with her. And she wasn't about to take no for an answer.

CHAPTER 7

Ten men were gathered together in the man cave. It dominated the basement of the mini mansion it was part of. The rest of the basement contained a laundry room, a hot water heater, and a water softener. The door to the man cave was closed and the men talked softly. They didn't want the wife of the master of the house to hear their conversation. They all knew she wouldn't approve of it if she did. And her disapproval could be incredibly difficult to live with. Especially since she was an accountant and the main breadwinner in the family. Top line accountants make a lot more money than cops.

"The trouble is," the cop, Silas Frederick, said, "is that we are going to have to be real damn careful with what and how we get to those people. I've done some pretty thorough checking on Lisa Thomas and the detective agency she manages. She isn't just ordinary folks that we can go willy-nilly after. None of those people are. According to everything I've been able to learn about them, they can be dangerous people to deal with."

Six of the men there, football players all, shook their heads and mumbled their opinions about his comments. Two other men, who were grown up football fans, just shrugged their shoulders.

Alger Gust, the defacto leader of the six men who chased Lisa and who were ultimately arrested, complained, "I don't think there's all that much they can do to stop us from teaching them a lesson after what that she bitch Lisa Thomas done to Jerry and Kelly. She only just got lucky with them. Otherwise, I don't think she coulda done to them what she done. Ain't no woman who could best any of us in a real fight. Besides, Jerry was the best high school quarterback in the state. We really need to get even for what she done. Otherwise, it's going to be pure hell trying to get the team spirit back where we need it. If we don't, we won't be winning many games this year."

"I guess you can believe what you want about them," Silas answered, "but it is in no way going to change the truth. And the truth is, those people up there in that Clayborne County are dangerous. They've been involved in a lot of things that would have beaten damn near anyone else, and come out on top every time."

"That shouldn't make no matter. All that matters is that they pay for what they done to our team. Everyone in our school was expecting us to be champions this season and she ruined it. There's a lot of disappointed folks who'd like to get some kind of satisfaction back. Having a disappointing football season is close to about as bad as life can get."

"I agree, Alger, that what's happened is a big disappointment. It still isn't going to change the fact that we have to think about what we try to do. And that means we can't just charge up there and attack those people. If we are going to do anything, we are going to have to carefully plan it."

"Maybe. But to start with, so all them disappointed people can get some satisfaction, why don't we go after them two women what started this whole deal."

"Which women are you talking about?"

"Them ones what say that Jerry and Glenn and us other four guys on the team was grabbing them and was going to do something bad to them. We was just fooling around, you know."

"What do you propose we do to them now?"

"We should grab 'em and do to them what they said we was goin' to do before. Maybe mess 'em up some while we do."

"The trouble with doing that is the fact that a lot of people will sympathize with them. That Melissa woman was told by her doctor that day that she has breast cancer. The one with her is her daughter. So going after them might not be the best idea. Everyone feels bad for a woman who might lose her tits."

"Well, without no doubt, we gots to go after someone. We can't just let them goddamn, stupid small town jerks get away with what they done. If we can't go after that Lisa bitch first, then let's raise some royal hell with that couple what rammed into Mister Smith's SUV when we was only just fooling with them women. They can't do nothing to stop us. He's so weak he can't even fight back. And she's just an ordinary bitch. Good looking enough to fuck, maybe. But still just an ordinary bitch."

"There's one big problem with your thinking, Alger. That guy is Lisa Thomas's dad. You do him any harm, and you will likely have her coming after you. Tough as you are, I don't think you want her after you. Not knowing what she did to Jerry and Kelly."

"From what Jerry said, Silas, she just got lucky. They wasn't suspecting it when she attacked them. If they'd of known what she was about, they'd of whipped her easy. I ain't got no doubts but what I can beat her in a fair fight."

The eight men who weren't quite able to express any kind of oral opinion about what should be done, shook their heads in agreement with Alger. After all, he was a six foot seven inch football player who weighed in at two hundred sixty pounds. How could any mere mortal woman ever do so much as one thing to harm him?

"I guess you can give it your best shot. The thing is, I'm going to have to stay out of it. With me being a cop, if things went wrong and I went to jail because of it, I'd have a much worse time of it than you ever would. And even if it didn't go wrong that way, I damn sure don't ever want my wife to find out I had any part of this. She's a women's libber from way back, and she'd goddamn well make me pay for it forever. And I damn sure would miss the way she spreads them long legs of hers for me."

Everyone there got a good laugh out of his comment about his wife. They all quietly agreed that it would not be a good thing to lose. Other than doing all the domestic things a woman was obligated to do, the willingness to spread their legs on demand was the most important thing a wife could do. In their opinions, any male who didn't know that wasn't a real man.

It was a belief that was reenforced everyday by the man who was the biggest hero to all ten of them. Donald Trump. A man who, they were sure, had shown the world the right way to treat women. Never mind that the adult, married males in their little group never treated their wives quite like Trump treated his. If they did, they would all quickly be divorced males.

Only the football players could sometimes get away with treating the girls they took out that way. And that's why, like it was with Trump, the only spread legs they ever had contact with was when there was a rape going on.

When the meeting of the ten broke up that evening, they were all somewhat satisfied with their plans. First, they would figure out how they were going to get at Bob Anderson in the rehabilitation clinic where he was still recovering from the beating they gave him. Once there, they'd give him another one.

That was to be followed with the abduction of his wife, Beth. They were sure they'd be able to break into her house at night, and take her from there. They had no idea as yet, that she would no longer be there.

CHAPTER 8

Bob Anderson was determined to be as little a burden to anyone as he possibly could. So from the minute he arrived at the rehabilitation clinic he worked hard to recover from his wounds and become ever more independent. He took it upon himself to exorcise way beyond what was expected of him.

From the start, he needed a walker to do it, but he managed to increase the time and length of his walks on an almost daily basis. He also increased the number of them. And because the hospital bed he slept in was acutely uncomfortable, he usually got up in the middle of the night and took one of his walks. That always seemed to loosen up his sore muscles and ease his pain enough to allow him to go back to sleep. If he didn't get up to walk, all he did was toss and turn for the rest of the night.

The first couple of times he got out of bed at around two AM, the night staff questioned his reasons for doing it, and were sure that he belonged in bed. Not up and wandering the halls of their facility. By the third night, they realized that he was going to be okay during his walk, and stopped interfering with it.

He was out on one of those walks when four men managed to creep undetected into his room. There were two beds in the room. One of them was empty but had obviously been slept in. That fact wasn't something that occurred to them. They were too anxious to beat the living hell out of what they thought was a helpless old man who had caused them problems. From their point of view, there was no excuse for him to interfere when they were about to have some fun with a couple of women. Even if the women didn't want their fun at the start, they were certain that they always loved it in the end. How could they not? What could be better fo a woman than sex with a football player. Why would they care if they were forced when it was football players doing it.

The old man in the occupied bed was sleeping on his side, with his back to them when they entered the room. They didn't hesitate, and immediately went after him with the baseball bats they brought with them.

Thinking it was Bob that they were beating on, they had no way of knowing that they were killing a ninety-three year old man. He had brittle bones, a bad heart, and two cracked ribs from a previous fall. The bats broke the ribs, and the sharp point of one of them moved enough to pierce the man's heart. He died several minutes before the beating stopped.

On this night, Bob was particularly uncomfortable. It was raining outside, and the moving barometer was raising hell with his arthritis. Arthritis he acquired primarily from years of bending while milking cows. So even though he was moving even slower than his normal slow walk, he decided to make an extra walk around. That brought him back to his room slightly less than two minutes after the four men decided they had damaged the body they were beating on enough.

As he went in, something about the room didn't feel right, so he did something he usually avoided. He turned on the light. The first thing he noticed was the water on the floor. He knew it was raining, but the water being where it was didn't made any sense. Not unless someone from the outside had come in and dripped on it.

He then looked at his roommate. Because he was covered, Bob had to look hard to see the telltale sign of blood on his top sheet. The four men had intentionally avoided hitting his head, so it was left unmarked. Bob put his hand on the man's shoulder to check on him. He moved closer to him and as soon as he looked at his face, Bob knew he was dead.

He picked up the button for calling someone when help was needed, then waited. It took a while for anyone to get there. This was a rehabilitation clinic that was chronically understaffed, and a place where there was only rarely any kind of an emergency, so the wait was normal.

The attendant who finally did come gave Bob a hard look and asked, "So what seems to be the problem tonight?"

"I think he's dead," Bob answered, pointing at his roommate.

"What the hell?" He looked close at the dead man, but almost seemed to be afraid to actually touch the body. "I guess I should tell someone."

It was obvious to Bob then that the man, who's job it was to be there to help, had no idea of what he was suppose to do. Bob pushed the nurse call button again and continued to do so until someone else finally joined them. This time it was a real nurse. She actually looked closely at the man and confirmed what Bob suspected.

As required by law, she called 911 to report the suspicious death. As soon as the deputy sheriff arrived and confirmed that the man appeared to be beaten to death, Sheriff Dale Magee was called. He was notified about it because he requested that they call him if anything unusual happened at the rehabilitation center while Bob was staying there.

After the attempted attack on Beth, he wanted to be on top of any unusual things that happened to either Beth or Bob. He had learned, from past events, that in situations like this it was always best to stay as involved as possible. If it came to it, it was always better to waste some extra effort then it was to not make it and have things end in disaster.

At the same time, he wished he didn't have to call Lisa about what just happened. The call would upset her. It couldn't do anything else. But he had no choice. She needed to know. So did Mack.

There was no hiding how they felt when they got there. Their anger was written all over their faces. They didn't know the dead roommate. They'd never done more than say hello to him. But they still felt very bad for him. At the same time, they had little doubt that Bob was the intended victim. They were also fairly certain about who the perpetrators were.

"Sometimes, Dale, it is about impossible to believe people can be driven to do something like this because of a game. A game that has less importance than the avocado crop in northern Minnesota."

"Given that there are no avocados ever grown in Minnesota, Mack, what you're saying is that football has zero importance."

"That's right. I am. Because it doesn't. It's a goddamn game. In reality, it has no direct affect on anyone's life. Except for those who play the game. No sport does. Not a positive one. As I've said before. All sports teach anyone is that for you to be successful, someone else must be unsuccessful. Real sportsmanship is actually rare. It mostly only exists in some coaches wet dream."

"I think you are pretty much right, Mack. But to most people, it really does matter who wins. The team wins, and they feel like they won something."

"That's my point. The people who support the team that loses, feel like they've lost. When the truth is, their real, actual lives are still the same. They might feel different, but it's a stupid, senseless feeling compared to what real life is about. And since at the end of any sports season there can be only one finale champion, all too many people end up depressed over something that just plain doesn't matter one fucking bit. And there's no better example to that than the situation we have right here. We have a completely innocent dead man, all because some sports people are upset because their star, rapist quarterback went after the wrong person and got himself hurt."

"I take it that you feel sure about who did this then?"

"Without a doubt, Dale. I know it's going to be damn hard to prove it, but those people from down there in the cities did it. I'm also sure that they'll continue to try to get even with us because of their quarterback."

Lisa, who was initially too concerned about her dad to say anything, finally spoke up. "I agree completely with Mack," she told Dale. "Those football players, along with some of their fans, think they're above the law. The only rules they believe they should have to follow are the rules of the game they play. And I'd guess they probably break some of them too. That means this crap is not going to go away. Which also means we will have to find someplace else for dad to stay. Anything public is now going to be too dangerous."

"I won't argue that," Dale said. "It's going to mean my entire department is going to have to be on full alert too."

"And all this shit is happening," Mack said, "because of some over privileged players believed they should be allowed to do whatever they want to do. Only because they play football."

"I can tell you both one thing," Lisa told them, leaving no doubt that she meant it, "I have no intention of sitting back and waiting for them to come after us. One way or the other, this shit is going to stop."

"I hope you don't plan on doing anything against them all on your own, do you?" Dale asked.

"Only if I have too. One way or the other though, like I told those assholes, this is war. And it's not one I intend to lose."

Mack felt much the same way she did. "You know I'll be with you every step of the way, Lisa. There's no way you're going after them alone."

Lisa shook her head no. "Not this time, Mack. I'll find a way to deal with this. You're going back to your work in the refuge. That's your job, and it's every bit as important as anything I'm going to be doing."

"I'm not so sure about that. I agree with you that the work we're doing to get the refuge to the place it should be is important. The trouble is, there's nothing in this world we live in more important to me than you are, Lisa. You know I'd rather let even the refuge die before I'd let something happen to you when I might be able to keep it from happening."

"I know how you feel, Mack," Dale said. "If there was something like this happening to Kathy," he added, talking about his wife, "I'd feel the same way. I'd try to do whatever it took to keep her from harm. At the same time, I would let you do with her what I'm now offering to do with Lisa. I've got a ton of vacation time coming. That means I can work with Lisa while she's trying to solve this problem. You going back to work in the refuge *is* that important."

Mack frowned. "I appreciate the offer, Dale, but given the relationship you have with Lisa, is your main reason for doing this to help her solve this problem? Or are there other motives?"

Dale had difficulty suppressing his laugh. "I have to admit, Mack, that when it comes to Lisa, yes, there are always those other motives. In this case though, I will first and foremost be there to assist her and offer what protection I can. And when it comes to that, there are things I can do for her that you can't. I am, after all, the sheriff of this county."

"I think what Dale wants to do is the best way to handle it," Lisa said. "And you don't have to worry about anything else, Mack. Until this is over, we will be concentrating on what needs to be done. Just like I expect that you will be concentrating on your work with Shanty in the refuge."

"Starting tomorrow," Mack answered, "I won't be able to do anything else during our normal hours there. The volunteer high school kids will be starting, and just giving them work direction will keep Shanty and me plenty busy."

"That's good. Just be sure that when I'm not home you and Shanty keep it to just relaxing with a beer at the end of the day. And when Kathy comes over and sits in your lap because she misses Dale, keep your clothes on."

"Sometimes, Lisa," Mack told her, "when you talk like that, you make me start thinking about my idea about giving up all that we have here and taking you away on that long trip I've talked about. Spending our time seeing new things, taking pictures, and writing about what we're doing. It would be a relief to forget the rest for a while."

"I know, Mack. I'm sorry. I know that sometimes things get way more complicated than what you'd like them to be. I wish I could change that right now. I just can't. Dad and Beth need us. The agency needs me to be there to keep it running. Shanty needs you in the refuge. Right now the refuge, if it's going to be what you've wanted it to be for so long, needs you to be there. And the truth of it is, getting that job done, even if it isn't going to change the whole world, is still really important. So if all this pushes me and Dale to what will probably be too close together sometimes, what you will be doing is too important for you to not go back to it."

"Okay, Lisa. We'll try it your way. For now. But if things get out of hand, it will only make all the problems we are facing just that much worse. So before you let that too closeness thing start, think about what it might do. For the four of us, me and you and Dale and Kathy, now is the time for all of us to remember who it is we really are."

"I agree with you, Mack," Dale told him. "I don't think I'd like it much if, when Lisa and I are working on this case, you and Kathy over did it either. What the four of us normally have is something we can all deal with. Pushing it the way it could be pushed, is only going to cause hurt all the way around."

"I guess I'm the weak one of us." Lisa tried to smile, but failed in the attempt. "I didn't think of it that way. I was thinking wrong. It's a good thing Mack is who he is, and understands me as well as he does. He knows better than anyone. Better than I do myself. How screwed up my thinking about things like this can be. And it was again this time. It could be again. So I expect that both of you, from time to time, need to remind me of that. It will be every bit as important as ending the harassment from those sports fans."

"I do expect you home, if not every night, at least most nights," Mack answered, "so you will be frequently reminded."

"And if for any reason, we need to stay in the cities some night," Dale added, "I'll remind us. Anything other than solving the problem we need to solve will have to wait."

This time Lisa did laugh. "Well then, on the nights we are home, Dale, you had better be nice to Kathy. And you, Mister Mack Thomas, had better go way beyond nice. Future temptation or not, I'll probably need that."

CHAPTER 9

Shanty was in a better mood at breakfast this morning than she'd been in since the trouble with Beth and Bob started. For her, the best thing of all was that Mack was going back to work in the refuge. Lisa was going to be working with Dale solving the problems with the people from the cities, and that was good news for her too.

They'd decided that rather than move Bob Anderson somewhere, they'd provide him with around the clock protection. Doing it in a timely matter would have been difficult for most people. It wasn't any problem for Mack and Lisa to do. They called Shanty that night, and because she owned a small company that provided the service, they had his first guard stationed there in record time.

Dale and Kathy were there to eat breakfast this morning. They didn't always join the group, but since Dale was going to be working so tightly with Lisa it seemed to be the right thing to do.

He knew that what he and Lisa were facing was a serious and possibly dangerous matter, and he was in a very somber mood. Kathy, on the other hand, was looking forward to spending extra time with Mack, and it left her, like Shanty, in a rather chipper mood.

Dale talked to her about the three of them deciding there must be some restrictions on any extra curricular activities, but she didn't care. Those things with Mack were great, but even without any of that, for her any and all time spent with him was special. The rules she was expected to follow while Dale and Lisa worked together were far more rigid than she thought they should be, but that didn't do anything to change her mood. Rules or not, during the time she might have with him she could still hold his hand and sometimes sit in his lap. She loved doing both, and either one of them filled a need in her like nothing else.

Lisa watched Kathy when she first came in. It wasn't difficult for her to see what she was thinking. She found it interesting that Kathy didn't appear in the least concerned about her and Dale working together the way they were going to. It was the same with her. She was neither concerned nor was she jealous about what Kathy and Mack might do during that time. She was used to Mack spending time with women who were in love with him. Shanty was a perfect example of it. That meant the tight rules they were to follow were all Dale and Mack. That might have upset her, if it weren't true that what it actually did was reassure her as to how much Mack loved her. So she knew she couldn't do anything to let him down. Those thoughts didn't put her into a particularly cheerful mood, but they did balance out her previously unsteady emotions.

Dale's mood was simple. Get Lisa through this coming ordeal as safely as he possibly could. He knew he would have his hands full the whole time. She had a strong tendency toward reckless behavior and he knew that was the major problem he was facing. He had to do everything in his power to keep her safe. Thoughts of their personal relationship were in a far distant place. He did wonder though, what Mack might be thinking at that point.

Mack was wondering the same thing about the other three. Lisa he knew, was mostly anxious to drive to the mall where it the first incident occurred, in order to try and learn more about the six men who started the trouble. Like Dale, their personal relationship was being pushed back into the far reaches of her mind. As far as she was concerned at that moment, anything other than solving the current problem and making everyone safe again, the other stuff did not matter enough to let it concern her.

It was easy to see that Kathy was seeing it all differently from the way he, Lisa, and Dale were. She had grown up a person that took most things in her life very seriously. Especially her music. She'd worked hard enough at it to become rich and famous. She still gave it her all when she made a recording or was giving a concert, but now approached it in a far more relaxed style. She no longer worried about her success or failure as a singer. She took life as it came to her, day by day. She always did her best to get as much from each and everything she did as was possible. She loved Dale and her time with him, and planned to keep him in her life for as long as her life lasted. But there was another part of her life she cherished above all else. Her time with Mack. So she grabbed it and held on tight whenever it was offered to her. It left no wonder then, why she was in such a good mood this morning. She knew for a little while, she'd have a little extra of that special treasure. Time with Mack.

Watching her, Mack picked up on what she was thinking and feeling. He knew her well enough to be able to read her moods with little difficulty. In one way it pleased him that she cared enough for him to feel the way she did. In another way, it disturbed him some. He knew that she wouldn't hold back through the coming ordeal as much as he would. It would take some effort on his part not to succumb to her likely willingness to ignore the rules.

The one saving grace in all of it was that while Lisa and Dale were working together, he would be very busy in the refuge. The whole time he was there, Shanty would be working with him. That would leave far less time for Kathy to work her mischief on him. Not that he minded what she did. Anything with her was a pleasure. It was just that he knew it must be kept in perspective. He knew without a doubt, his first commitment was to Lisa, as was Kathy's to Dale.

As all those thoughts ran through Mack's mind, he was blissfully unaware of the way he was being watched. It didn't occur to him that the three women now playing such a prominent role in his life would be paying extremely close attention to his expression. Even if he was, he was equally unaware of how much his expression told each of them.

That meant they knew of his concern about his relationship with each of them. At least as much, if not more, than he did. Their awareness of what his concerns were, left them with all the feelings they had previous to the decision that Dale and Lisa would be working together, and their doing so would leave Mack with free time when Lisa was busy.

They were now at a point where Mack, if he had the same dubious character as all too many men, could have taken advantage of the situation. He wasn't about to do that. He held all of them to too high a level to even consider such a thing.

Instead, he was anxious to get to the refuge and go to work. All of the actual construction being done now, was done by professional builders of various kinds. Water control structures and maintenance roads were the top of the list of the refuge's projects.

Shanty had spent enough of her billions on land acquisitions to have more than doubled the size of the refuge. It was now somewhat larger than the original refuge that was put together by the federal government. The portion of the refuge that was lost so Lands Magnificent could build their resort was still a resort. All the land added to it this time was acquired to the north and west of it.

Most of the land they'd purchased was previously small farmsteads, along with many private homes. Nearly four thousand acres of the land had been hunting preserves. There were a lot of homes, barns and other structures on the new land. Since human built structures like houses and barns had nothing to do with the natural world, they were now being bulldozed down, and their remains buried where they once stood. That work was nearly completed. Also nearing completion was the seeding of native grasses on the open ground that was once farm fields.

Another major project that was just getting underway, and the one Mack and Shanty were currently managing, was the construction of hiking trails. The bulk of the physical work involved in creating them was going to be done by volunteer students from the high school.

It was a task he, along with Shanty, was not looking forward to. Having hiking trails were not something he was in favor of. Having as many as were planned was something he didn't like at all. Even if he did know they were required. They were needed in order to keep the publics interest in the refuge. Without it there would be far fewer of the financial donations which would be needed to keep the refuge going in the future.

A second part of the trail building they were dreading was working with the high school kids. Mack had worked with some of them in the past, but always felt somewhat out of touch with most of them. Shanty had little to no experience with them.

Even when they, themselves were teenagers, they'd had little to do with other kids. Shanty had been homeschooled by a teacher her father hired. It was considered, because of her father's wealth, unsafe for her to attend public, or even any private, school.

Mack's teenage years were primarily spent working with his father, roaming the wildlife refuge they lived next to, and riding the half wild horse Roy gave him. He got along okay with other kids, and did passably well in school, but normal teenage activities were never his primary interests.

It meant they were left with what felt like a foreign world for them to deal with. A world they'd strongly considered avoiding. Were they less dedicated to the huge project they'd undertaken, they probably would have. They knew though, that nearly as important part of the refuge as preserving part of the earth and providing homes for millions of creatures, was using it to educate people about the environment. They knew too, in the long term, the best place to concentrate that effort was with the young.

To get the student volunteers, they worked with teachers and councilors in the high school. The principle of the school, Don Locks, who worked with Mack in the past, worked especially hard to convince as many students as possible to volunteer. He even set up a program so the kids got credit for the work they did. Something that would help any of them get into a college of their choice.

It didn't seem to have mattered much though. Teenagers now seemed to be far more interested in their version of communicating with their cell phones, playing video games, and hanging out at the mall, then they were in doing anything outdoors. Especially anything requiring hard physical work. So their expectation was for a small turnout of kids who were incessantly called nerds and other names. Some of which could be unkind.

When the bus arrived at what was now the headquarters of the expanded refuge, they were pleasantly surprised. Fifteen kids got off it. The downside of that was three of them. All boys, who were sure they were as macho as any male could get. They were obvious enough about it to make Mack think about Lisa, and wonder how she was doing in her investigation of the problem football players and their fans.

As much as he wanted to, he couldn't let his thoughts linger with her. Not with fifteen teenagers waiting for some kind of work direction. One of the boys, who appeared to be the leader of the three questionable ones, didn't hesitate to show Mack his impatience with the whole deal.

He glared at Mack. "What the hell are we supposed to do, now that we're here in this half-assed jungle for stupid animals. Ain't none of us what came here to stand around waiting. Not even them nerds, stupid as all of them are."

"I think in your case," Mack quickly answered, "the best thing *you* can do is get back on the bus. So do it quick, before it leaves. I'd hate for me or my partner Shanty here, to have to haul you back into town. And if you stick around, that's likely what will happen. With your attitude, you and I are highly unlikely to get along well enough to work together."

"Well, don't you think you're hot shit. I don't think you're nobody to talk to me the way you just done. I'm here 'cause my dad wants me here. He said what all you people here are doing is wrong. I'm here to help him prove that, and he said there ain't a damn thing you can do about it. Not after you went to the school and asked for volunteers. After you done that, you got to let me stay. Else he can sue you."

Mack had a head full of things he could have told the kid, but decided it would only be a senseless gesture. So would sending him back to town. Instead, Mack decided the best way to deal with the kid would be to put him to work. Especially any and all difficult and heavy work they were bound to encounter as they built the new hiking trails.

Of all the kids there, this young version of a macho male probably needed the kind of education Mack was about to give him more than all the rest of the kids combined.

When Mack didn't tell the kid to get back on the bus, Shanty cocked her head to one side, raised her eyebrows, and said to Mack, "Really? You are really going to do this?"

Mack shrugged. "We have to try. Just because everyone else has given up on him, doesn't mean we have to. If it proves to be impossible, I'll be the one to give him a ride back to town."

They made no attempt to keep the kid from hearing them, and he didn't like what they said about him. "Ain't nobody given up on me," he said, working hard to put a snarl in his voice, "so you and the bitch here can watch what you say about me."

"If you call me a bitch again," Shanty told him, "I'm going to take you over my knee and paddle your sorry ass."

That comment brought on giggles and laughter from the rest of the kids. His two buddies as well as the nerds.

It was then that one of the female students spoke up. "I think that it would be a good for you guys to just put him back on the bus.

He's Teddy Nichole. He talks all the time about how much his dad hates you guys. He used to have a farm someplace here that you guys bought from him. Teddy keeps saying you cheated him. Their farm was worth more than you paid them for it."

What she said once again reminded Mack of one of the main problems they faced as they turned all of the recently acquired private land into a public wildlife refuge. The land itself was still privately owned, but rather than being used by only a few people when it was farmed or used for hunting, it was now going to be something the public could use.

The problem was that even though every piece of ground they purchased was bought at a price higher than the market value of the land at the time, many of the previous owners still resented those responsible for expanding the refuge. It didn't matter how much they got for their land, they felt they should have gotten more.

Teddy Nichole's father was near the top of the list of the worst of them. His attitude was made even worse by the fact that he was an addicted gambler, and had lost a good part of the money from the sale of his farm at the casino. In doing so, he drove his wife and their daughter out of his life. Now all he had left was an ancient mobile home sitting on an acre of land that was on the verge of becoming part of nearby wetlands.

He still managed to put in a full days work on a construction crew as a laborer every day, but it was a rare day he did it without a hangover. Mack, of course, didn't know all that yet, but did suspect something like it. So he made the decision to try and work with Teddy. As much as he wanted to simply dump him by putting him back on the bus, he knew deep inside that if he could get through to the kid, he was probably worth salvaging. Added to that, if he did get through to him, the world might have one less person like those Lisa was right now hunting.

Shanty, who was watching Mack go through the mental struggles as he tried to decide what to do with Teddy, finally told him what he needed to hear. "You're right, Mack. Let him stay. For now anyway. It does, after all, seem to be your mission to save so many of the outcasts in life. You are doing a lot good by working so hard to make this a refuge restored. It's more than most ever accomplish in a lifetime. Yet, here you are, about to try to save another of us errant souls. The things you do sometimes, Mack, does give me hope for the human race. It also tells me that if only there were more like you, this world would be one hell of a lot better place."

Along with the other fourteen kids there, Teddy was again listening to them talk. And like them, he was now wondering about the man who they were going to be working with. He appeared so different. He was a fairly big man, and had some old scars on his face. He wore cowboy style clothes, and wore a western hat. But his face showed a simple kind of caring they rarely saw. It settled some of the anxiety they were all feeling, and they quietly followed Mack and Shanty to the trail they would be working on this day.

CHAPTER 10

Mack was more than satisfied with the day they had working with the kids. At the same time, he was happy to have it over. They'd gotten a good start, in spite of all of them tripping over each other. It was going to take, he knew, several days working together before things smoothed out.

His biggest concern with them was Teddy. He constantly attempted to dominate the work, which only made it more difficult. Nearly all of the other kids were better at nearly any task then he was. Especially the girls. They weren't as strong as the boys. They thought through each task more carefully when it was necessary to do so, and because they did, they often accomplished more things faster.

Mack was going through the work they'd be doing tomorrow when Shanty joined him on his deck. Like him, she was enjoying a cold can of beer.

"You're alone," she said. "Is Lisa staying in town tonight?"

"It's possible. She said when she called that they were watching four of those football players, who were in turn checking out a group girls. The girls looked like they weren't quite old enough for high school yet. Lisa and Dale were hoping to catch the players getting out of line with them. So they were going to continue watching. Whether or not they come home tonight will depend on how late it gets."

"I guess that's important, Mack. But I kind of wonder if it's worth it. I know it's important to protect Beth and Bob, I'm just not so sure having her and Dale out hunting the way they are is the best solution."

"I'm not either. The trouble is, I think I'd be wrong if I tried to tell her she can't do it."

"Aren't you worried about her though. There's a hell of a lot of things that could happen with her out and about the way she is. Especially with Dale being her partner in what she's doing."

Mack wasn't exactly sure what Shanty was referring to, so he hesitated before answering her. "I don't know what you mean, when you say so many things could happen to her with Dale?"

"Look, Mack, I know that you and Lisa have something special with Dale and Kathy. I can understand it, and I have nothing bad to say about it. I just wonder if it's such a good thing for them to be off by themselves the way they are now. They get into some high stress situations and get the adrenaline pumping, it can lead to all sorts of situations."

"I know. I still have trust her to use good judgement. Dale too. Not to mention, they aren't the biggest danger." He pointed out to the meadow they had preserved behind their house. "That danger is on her way here now."

Shanty followed Mack's finger and quickly spotted Kathy headed their way. She chuckled. "Well, I guess that does even things out a bit. Lisa's got Dale to worry about. You're about to have a second predatory female to be careful with."

"What do you mean, second predatory female?"

"Don't be coy, Mack. You know damn good and well what I'm talking about. It would take damn near no effort on your part to have your way with either one of us right now. With Lisa gone somewhere with Dale, it opens up things in a way they otherwise wouldn't be. You know I'm every bit as much in love with you as Lisa and Kathy are."

"Yes, and I love you too. It's just that I've never considered you as being at all predatory. More than that, you are mostly as good a friend as I could ever ask for."

"I hate to disappoint you, but I am one of those females. At times like this, I can't help wishing I could force myself on you. Hells, bells, right now I might even be willing to share you with Kathy. Something like that would never work with Lisa, I'm sure, but I can see it happening with her."

Kathy, who was starting up the steps on to the deck asked, "What can you see happening and with *who?*"

Mack laughed and Shanty blushed. "It's probably best I don't answer that question," she answered.

"Really," Kathy said as she sat on Mack's lap. "If that's the case, then you've definitely got my curiosity. You said something about sharing. What kind of sharing?"

"Are you sure you want me to answer that?"

"Damn right I am. I can't see any reason for you not too."

"Other than it's embarrassing, you're probably right." Shanty looked at Mack and waited until their eyes met. "What do you think, Mack? Should I tell her."

"I would say no if it wasn't because the two of you won't give up on the subject until you do. So go ahead. Tell Kathy what you said."

Shanty was smiling now. Since there was no way what she was going to tell Kathy was going to happen, she thought it was best to keep it light hearted. "I just told Mack that since Lisa wasn't home, and she was with Dale, it now made him fair game for us predatory females. I also told him that if it was the only way to do it right now, I'd be willing to share him with you."

Kathy didn't show any negative reaction to what Shanty said. Instead, she kissed Mack first, then smiled and answered, "Do you think we could talk him into it?"

Mack tried to take what was said in stride, but found himself physically reacting to Kathy's comment. He also blushed.

Because she was on his lap, Kathy could feel his strong reaction. Taking advantage of the situation, she wiggled against him. Her moves told Shanty what Kathy's comment was doing to Mack.

"I think," Shanty said, "as much as it would be a hell of a lot of fun, it's time to shut this down. All three of us know that if we followed through with this, it would probably lead to disaster. I for one, do not want to in anyway mess up what Mack and Lisa have."

Kathy gave Mack one more wiggle, sighed, then agreed. "I don't either. Not really. Not to mention, Dale and I promised each other to keep things on the straight and narrow until after the problem down in the cities is settled."

"Thank you both for that," Mack told them. "We do have to keep things cool until Lisa and Dale get done what they need to get done. At the same time, I have to tell you. The thought of being in bed with the two of you at the same time is almost more than my poor heart can take."

"Well then," Kathy said, "maybe we'll consider it sometime in the future. Who knows, Lisa and Dale might like the idea too."

"Two men and three women," Shanty said. "It's hard to say whether that would be exciting or just crowded."

"Enough you two," Mack argued. "We aren't going to do anything about any of those things, so let's talk about something else. If I don't get my mind where it belongs, sleep is going to be hard to come by tonight."

"I would imagine," Kathy teased, "sleeping wouldn't be the only hard thing around tonight."

Mack did his best to ignore her. "What," he asked Shanty, "did you think about the kids today? Are we ever going to get then to the point they actually work together?"

His question once again caught Kathy's curiosity. "What are you talking about all the sudden? What kids working?"

Shanty answered her. "Today, fifteen high school kids started working with us, building trails. For the most part, they tried their best. It's just that they were very uncoordinated with everything they did."

"That they were," Mack agreed. "Especially the three macho boys."

"You've got to admit though, Mack, they wouldn't have been quite so bad if we'd have sent Teddy back on the bus."

"Who's Teddy and what's this about sending him back on the bus?" Kathy asked.

"Most of the kids working with us," Shanty explained, "are the ones who are in school primarily to get an education. Three of them are boys who think they are, or at least should be, god's gift to all the girls they ever get near. One of them is particularly obnoxious. Mack came close to sending him back to town on the bus that brought him to us. Then he changed his mind. So now we have working with us, someone who is going to be a rather large pain in the ass. Someone who, nonetheless, Mack is determined to do his best to save."

Kathy chuckled. "That's Mack. Always saving someone. But that's a good part of why we love him the way we do. It would be damn hard to find a better man than him. Everyone who knows him would be less without knowing him."

"I couldn't agree more. The truth is, he's the only man I feel totally comfortable with. I grew up with a very abusive father, married a man nearly as bad, and lived with a heavy drinking, cheating mother. Being able to spend most of my time now with a man like him is a real godsend. It would be difficult for life to get any better for me. And we all know what that would be."

"Yes, it's just that one thing." Kathy grinned and a devilish gleam flashed in her eyes. "I think, somewhere down the line, we are going to have to fix that. No matter what anyone ever says about right or wrong, you should sometime have at least one night alone with Mack. Maybe even more than one."

"Don't I have anything to say about that?" Mack asked.

"Sure, but would you actually object, if it could happen without hurting Lisa or me?"

"Probably not, but…"

"There you have it. You just had your say. How about you, Shanty? Would you object to that?"

"Me? Object to my dream night in heaven? I don't think so." She smiled, even with a couple of tears rolling down her cheeks.

CHAPTER 11

The girls Dale and Lisa were watching left their table and started picking up their many packages. They'd had a busy day shopping. The football players who were watching the girls, hadn't as yet made any moves on them, but they left their table too. As they did, they left little doubt that they intended to follow the girls out of the mall.

Dale and Lisa didn't have to say or do anything. It went without saying, they would be following both groups until the girls were safely in their cars or on a bus, on the way home. Then came something they didn't expect. Two full grown men joined the players.

They were dressed like blue collar workers. One was wearing some kind of uniform, and the other a dark blue teeshirt and jeans. Their movements were off just enough to tell Lisa and Dale that they'd been drinking. There was no way to know what their intentions toward the girls were, but the situation looked serious enough to continue watching them.

It was not at all what Lisa and Dale wanted to be doing. They were already a lot later going home than they wanted to be, and this was going to make them that much later. They still planned to go home when it was over, no matter how late it got, knowing that it was the best thing they could do. No matter how late it was or how tired they were.

If they stayed in the cities, even in separate rooms, it would not be accepted well at home. Neither Mack nor Kathy would complain. They'd just always wonder, did they stay because it was so late and they were tired? Or were there other reasons? Lisa most of all didn't want Mack to wonder. Not when he had that something inside him that often told him he was holding her back. That he wasn't always good enough, and maybe her life would be better if he got out of her way. She knew she could lose him simply because of that. It was something that she knew was impossible. Without him, everything in her life would be much less, never better. So this time, she was going to make sure she didn't send him the wrong signal by staying in town.

As she and Dale followed the players and men following the girls, her thoughts were about what she was doing. Perhaps, when this night was finally done, she should back off at least for a while from trying to hang the football players and their fans who were after Beth and Bob. Whatever it was that happened with this group should be enough for now.

Before she could come to any kind of firm decision, the girls reached the van they'd come in. It was old enough to need a key to unlock the doors, so the men and players caught up with them before they got inside it. They didn't hesitate to let the girls know what they wanted.

As they did, they made no attempt to charm the girls, or to otherwise convince them to yield to their desires. The men and the boys all simply acted as if they were Donald Trump and started grabbing. Like it always was for Trump when it came to females, rape was the name of the game. And like him, the age of the females didn't matter. All that mattered was them taking what they wanted from the girls.

Lisa and Dale, of course, weren't about to allow it to happen. To better deal with the men and boys, who out numbered them six to two, they moved several feet apart as they drew their weapons. Six of the seven girls were struggling hard against the male attackers. The seventh girl was using crutches, and had a brace on one leg. She leaned against the van, dropped one crutch and grabbed the other one by its bottom. She swung it as hard as she could, hitting one of the grown men on the temple. The blow was hard enough to leave a gash where it landed. That was followed by a nice steady flow of blood. He went down and stayed there.

That action inspired Lisa. She holstered her gun and approached the largest of the football players. She tapped his shoulder and shook her head no. He thought he'd struck it rich. Here was this beautiful woman standing in front of him, ready for the taking. And taking her was exactly what he intended to do. He didn't get far.

On is first reach for her she grabbed his wrist, used her arms and the rest of her body to spin him around. With his arm trapped behind him, she broke it, then stepped back. her foot, covered by her western style boot, slammed into the side of his right knee. It made a loud snapping sound as it was also broken. He dropped to the ground. While she was busy, Dale took out the other players.

That left the last man standing. He was in a bit of a daze as he tried hard to understand what had just happened. How the hell could these two people take down four big and strong football players so easily? And that little girl with the crutches? His friend was still laying there on the ground. He was still bleeding and it was obvious he wasn't getting up anytime soon.

Lisa held up her hand to Dale, telling him to stay where he was. She moved up close to the man. "It's like this," she said, "you can either get down on your knees to these girls and beg their forgiveness for what you thought you were going to do. Or, you can take your chances with me, and me alone. I will promise you though, that if you do take me on, I will show you no quarter. If you survive, only an ambulance will take you away."

"Your friend's gonna stay out of it?"

"You have my word on that. It's just you and me."

"Well damn," he smirked, "this is gonna be fun."

It wasn't. Lisa didn't just fight him. She tortured him. She took out on him all the aggression built up inside from a long and tedious day. As she did, there was an unreal silence surrounding her and her punching bag. She purposely didn't knock him out. She wanted him aware of every small bit of pain she inflicted on him.

When she finished with him, she pulled him to a sitting position. Moving within inches of his face she said, "If you ever go after another girl in your life, you'd best remember what I just did to you. Because if I ever find out you did anything even remotely like this, I will find you. When I do, I will inch by tiny inch, turn you into a very messy dead body. Then I will take pictures of it, so that everyone you ever knew can see how you died." She shook him some to be sure she had his attention. "Do you understand me?"

It was a feeble gesture when he shook his head yes. It wasn't enough to satisfy Lisa. She shook him again, harder this time. "Now I want you to say how sorry you are to all these girls." She waited for him to say it. When he didn't, she slapped his face. "Tell them, or so help me god, I will make the pain you have now seem like nothing. Because if you don't apologize right now, I'm going to cut your nuts off." She shook him again.

He lifted his head, his eyes now filled with fear. "I'm so sorry," he said, his voice only slightly above a mumble. "I promise I won't do it again."

Lisa still wasn't satisfied, but decided to leave it at that. She gave him a final shake, then pushed him so he was flat on the ground. "And stay there," she ordered him. He did.

When she looked up at them, the seven girls were watching her with rapt attention. "I think," she told them, "that it's time you girls got in that van of yours and go home. We are all done here."

"Don't you think," one of the girls asked, "that we should call the police?"

"No." Lisa grimaced. "Here, they aren't much more than a pain in the ass. So do yourselves and us a favor and get the hell out of here. We are tired and just want to go home. You get the police involved and it'll just mean trouble for all of us. The four boys on the ground around us are football players."

The girl who asked about the police returned Lisa's look with a frown. She turned to her friends. "This lady is right. Let's go home. These creeps can be the ones to call the police."

Lisa and Dale waited for them to get out of the parking lot, then left it themselves. It was a quiet ride as Dale drove them home. When Dale dropped her off there, he asked, "Are we doing it again tomorrow?"

"I don't know," she answered. "Call me in the morning and we'll talk about it. I'm way too tired tonight to even think, let alone figure out what to do tomorrow."

Dale shook his head yes to tell her he understood. She moved slow when she went in the house. As she did she found herself thankful to Mack for leaving the door unlocked. She dropped her stuff on a side table near the door and went directly into the bedroom. She decided she would shower in the morning. She was simply too tired to do it tonight. When she crawled in next to Mack, all she was wearing was her skin.

He was awake and took her in his arms. In a minute his body told her how happy he was to have her home, safe and sound. She kissed him, then pulled herself over him. She wasn't too tired to be ready for him. She was. She moved her knees up, took him in her hand, and guided him inside. It only took them minutes to reach their mutual satisfaction before they were ready for sleep. The tension they'd carried all day was gone now. They closed their eyes.

Mack knew then, that whatever Lisa did now, it was going to be okay.

CHAPTER 12

Mack was up and out of the house long before Lisa was awake. He ate a quick breakfast while answering questions about what Lisa was doing. He let Shanty answer most of the questions about how the work was coming in the refuge. He wanted everyone, including her, to know what an important role she was playing in everything they were doing. More than that, he truly did believe that she answered those questions better than he did.

It wasn't until they were on the way to the refuge that she asked the question that was worrying her since she said goodnight to Mack the night before. "Is everything okay with you and Lisa? It was awful late when I left you last night, and she wasn't home yet."

"We're fine. She'll tell me why she was so late when she gets home tonight, if it isn't quite so late again."

"Well, good. I was hoping it would be okay. Like I've told you before, I would hate it if anything was to ever come between you two."

Mack gave her a quick look. "I know what you're worried about. There was nothing like that. Whatever made her late, it had something to do with her reason for being there."

"Good. I'm glad you're so sure." It was easy for Mack to hear the doubt in her voice.

He suppressed a smile, but kept a light tone to his voice. "There are ways to be sure, Shanty. Last night, those ways were used. I'm sure. You can stop worrying about it. Lisa was a good girl. Until she got home anyway."

"Okay, Mack," she agreed. She couldn't help herself and chuckled. "I won't say anymore." But she did feel some light pangs of jealousy. If anyone would have asked her who was the richest person in the world, she would have answered, "*Lisa.*"

They got to the headquarters early enough to get everything ready that they would need for the days work ahead of them. When the bus with the kids arrived, Mack watched closely to see who and how many got off it. He was sure there would be fewer than the previous day. All of the kids had done actual physical work, and he was sure that at least some of them would be unwilling to put in another day of the same thing.

He was pleasantly surprised when all fifteen of them got off the bus. His biggest surprise was Teddy. Mack didn't think there was much chance of his returning. He did his best the previous day to show everyone that he thought the work they were doing was trivial. A total waste of time. From his point of view, nothing in this refuge had any value. If it wasn't something directly beneficial for humans, it couldn't possibly be worth anything. When it was farmland it was valuable. Now it was worth little to nothing, as was everything that lived on this land.

"You know," Teddy said to one of the girls in the group, hoping to impress her, "that the only way working this hard here could make any sense would be if we were getting the land ready to plow, so we could plant corn or some other real crop. Building a trail just so some kind of dumb people can walk around looking at animals and trees. It don't make no sense."

"I think, Teddy," the girl who planned to go to college and study wildlife management answered, "it depends on how a person sees things. Some of us need, love, and respect the wild places and what lives in them. We need them as much as we need farms. They feed the mind and the soul, just like food feeds the body. When you think there is only one thing in life that really matters, I have to wonder if you're just missing something, or is something missing in you."

Teddy was just smart enough to know that it would make little sense to argue with her. He was hoping to somehow impress her and arguing with her wouldn't do that. Most of all, any argument he might make did have some missing parts. He didn't know or understand much of anything about the environment, the wildlife refuge, or even the needs, wants, or wishes of anyone but himself.

The rest of the day, they worked hard and even managed to work together occasionally. At the same time, Mack and Shanty always allowed them to stop and look at or even study the numerous creatures or interesting plants that they saw. The only one of them who refused to be at all impressed by the myriad of life around him was Teddy. Even when, at their midday meal when a small herd of deer moved in close to them, he pretended to not be interested. His only response was a comment about seeing herd of cows there would be better than a group of overgrown pests.

The one thing that captured his attention then was when Lisa stopped by to see Mack. One look at her, and she had his undivided attention. The girl he'd earlier hoped to impress noticed. She avoided him for the rest of the day. For her, the idea that he looked at an older woman like Lisa, beautiful or not, the way he did just wasn't right or fair as far as she was concerned.

At the same time, Lisa was completely oblivious to Teddy's stares. She was there to see Mack. It was time, she knew, for them to talk about a better way to deal with the problem with the people who were still out to hurt Beth and Bob.

"I thought you and Dale would be down in the cities," Mack said as soon as he saw her.

Lisa took his arm and pulled him away from the kids. She didn't want them listening to her and Mack. "I decided that after it go so late yesterday we should take a day off. I don't know either, if we're going to accomplish what we want to by doing what we were doing yesterday. I know you're busy now, so I won't stay here long. Mostly I came to tell you that no matter what we do, I'd feel better if I was doing it with you."

"Did Dale do something wrong?"

"No, Mack. Dale did good. It's just that it doesn't feel quite right to be doing what I was doing, the way I was doing it."

"What is it about it that's bothering you?"

Lisa looked at the ground and the foot she was sliding around in the dirt. She struggled to control her feelings before she answered him. "It's you, Mack. I'm scared about you. I'm afraid that if I keep on doing what I'm doing something will go wrong. When it does, you might get those ideas about you being in my way and you wanting to let me go, so I can do what I want. That's what scares me, Mack. Losing you. No matter what the reason might ever be, it would be the worst thing that could ever happen to me. What I want most in the world is what I have. Being with you."

"But you're not going to lose me, Lisa. You mean everything to me."

"I know. But because you are who you are, you might leave me anyway. Just to give me something you think you can't. The problem is, you give me everything, and without you I don't have a damn thing. So we have got to talk tonight about how to deal with this stuff without me going again to the cities with Dale or anyone but you."

"Okay, Lisa, we will talk about it tonight. When we do though, I think we should have Dale, Kathy, and Shanty part of the talk. I'm sorry to have to tell you this, but these kids are ready to go back to work."

Lisa smiled to let him know that she was okay with that. She kissed him, then left him to do what he needed to do. She still felt some stress when she got home, but a quiet afternoon hoeing a field of peppers for Ben worked away most of it. It left her hoping the work Mack was doing was helping him in the same way.

For him, the work itself was always an asset. Dealing with fifteen teenagers was a two way street though. It was sometimes very satisfying when they learned something new or accomplished a difficult task. Especially when they did it on their own. At the same time, some of the simplest things could seem to them to be impossible and drive the work to a standstill. Having it all too often necessary to intervene was something that could and did stress Mack.

Teddy's constant comments about stopping when ever they did it to watch some new or interesting creature also bugged him. He was frequently tempted to tell the kid to shut the hell up. The only reason he didn't was because he still hoped to get through to him, and teach him the value of the environment in general and places like the refuge in particular. It was what he wanted everyone to learn. If people could get out of themselves and learn about life beyond their own, it would be a better world.

It was about an hour before quitting time when things changed for all of them. Mack and Shanty were shocked to see it happen. They never thought she'd visit with all the kids around. It was something hey hoped she wouldn't do.

The kids went beyond shock and had trouble believing their own eyes. More than that, what they were seeing scared the daylights out of them. Seeing a bear walk in among them went beyond anything they would have ever imagined.

Speaking just loud enough to be heard, Mack told them, "Please stay quiet and don't move. She's not here to hurt anyone, but we don't want to startle her. If we stay calm, she will just say hello, then be on her way. But you all must stay calm."

The bear moved close to Shanty first, and stood up and touched her shoulders with her front paws. Their eyes met for a few moments before she dropped down and moved to Mack. With him, she pulled him close when her paws landed on his shoulder. She held him there for a while. As she did, she made a kind of contented growl. She let Mack scratch her behind the ears before she left him.

She then did the totally unexpected and checked the kids out, one by one. She didn't touch them until she reached Teddy. As she pushed her nose up close to his stomach, then touched his shoulder with a paw. He just stood there, totally mesmerized by her. He grinned as he realized what an awesome creature she was. In that moment he began to understand the value of the place he'd been so sure was worthless. It was like his life was moving from a known path to a new one, much like the trails they were building.

The bear gave a small shake of her head, turned then, and total silence followed her until she disappeared in the brush she came out of. When the kids talked, they all talked at once. All of them but Teddy. He didn't make a sound. He sat down on the ground slowly moving his head back and forth. With his mouth open, his eyes were as wide as was possible.

Mack studied him as Shanty tried to answer a barrage of questions. He waited until things started to quiet down, then told them what he knew he had to make them understand.

"What you all just saw was something extremely unusual. That bear is the one who decided to be friendly with us. For some unknown reason, she trusts us. But now we have a problem. It will be a very bad thing if anyone else besides all of us know about her and what she just did. Especially people who love to hunt. If the wrong ones learn about her, all they're going to want to do is come in this refuge and kill her. So I'm going to have to ask all of you to not say anything to anyone about what you saw here today. If you do, I am really very much afraid of what could happen to her. Not to mention, most of your parents are highly unlikely to let you come back."

"What Mack is telling you is true," Shanty added. "If you tell anyone about her, she will be in grave danger, as will your chances of continuing to work here. What we're going to have to do now, is catch her so we can have her moved somewhere far from here. If we don't get her moved, it's a sure thing that someone will hunt her and kill her."

The kids then agreed to keep silent about seeing her. Especially Teddy. A simple touch of his shoulder changed his world.

CHAPTER 13

Mack found himself with two big problems to deal with that evening. He was having a great deal of difficulty deciding which of them he should give priority too. He knew that if he didn't continue to spend his days at the refuge, there would be a much bigger chance of something bad happening to the bear than there would be if he was there.

At the same time, he knew that Lisa was going to ask him to partner up with him in her search for better ways to protect Beth and Bob. Disappointing Lisa wasn't something he wanted to do either. He was left feeling as though it didn't matter what he did. No matter what he chose to do, it would leave something important undone.

He knew he would need to find a solution to both problems, even if it seemed as though there were none. So instead of meeting with only Lisa, Dale, Kathy, and Shanty, he invited everyone living on the four hundred acre ranch/farm over for a visit after the evening meal. He waited for all of them to be settled comfortably down with the beverage of their choice before he said anything.

He started by telling them about the bear and what she'd done that day. He then explained to them about his concern for her and about how much he feared for her life. From there, he gave them a brief review of the danger Bob and Beth were in, and the need to bring that to an end.

Mack let them discuss what he'd told them for a few minutes, then he talked about the part that was more difficult to talk about. Lisa's concern about how he would end up reacting if she continued to to deal with the city people with someone other than him.

Kathy was the first to comment on that. "I don't blame Lisa at all for her concern. If Mack and I were to do something like she and Dale are doing, I would worry some about what Dale thought about it too. If they were on a normal kind of investigation, I think it would be different. But this one has too many things involved, and too many things could go wrong. So this time she's right in wanting Mack for her partner."

Dale was next. "After yesterday, I have to agree with Kathy. I thought when I volunteered to work with Lisa, that there'd be no problems. We'd worked together a lot in the past without any. This is different. Mack should be the one with her."

"I can't argue that point one way or the other," Shanty said. "But we still have one hell of a big problem in the refuge. You two are probably right about Mack being the right one to go with Lisa. The thing is, Mack's also the one who should be in the refuge to protect the bear. He's the one she truly trusts. And to save her, I have no doubt that we will need her to trust us. We have to somehow get her the hell out of there and too someplace far away and safe."

"Aren't there people who do that kind of thing?" Wanda asked. "Can't they handle the bear on their own."

"They normally could, yes. The trouble is, this bear is no longer completely wild. Because of that, she's more wise to what we are doing, and is going to be shy of any moves we make toward her. Especially with strange people involved. So far, she's initiated all the contact we've had with her. And that's only been when Mack was there. When he isn't there, she more or less avoids all of us."

Lisa was now feeling as if she was letting everyone down. Her concern about her relationship with Mack was real. Yet she still thought she was being selfish be expecting him to leave the refuge to work with her. Not to mention that the life of the bear might depend on his being there.

"I wish," she said, "I could feel different about this. I love Dale. He's as good a friend as I've ever had. I've worked with him a lot, and it's always been a positive experience. It's just that this time, when my coming home so late has kept Mack awake, I think it's best if it's him I work with. Yet, I'm as concerned about the bear as Mack is. She has every right to keep on living, the same as us. So as bad as I want him with me, I think it's more important they he stay in the refuge."

"I do too," Ben said. "Other than being married to you, Lisa, it's the most important thing he can possibly be doing. Especially since there are other ways of protecting Beth and Bob. There's a bunch of us, Lisa, who can work with you to protect them. Mack's the only one who can work with the bear the way she needs to be worked with. He also knows the refuge better than anyone else, be they trained to do that work or not. So regardless of what else anyone decides, next time you go down to the cities looking for solutions to the problems with your dad and Beth, I will be going with you. Mack knows damn good and well that I'd sooner die a hundred times than to see any harm come your way."

Roy then smiled in the way only Roy could smile. He said, "Me too."

Wanda laughed. "It figures. We started with a serious problem. Now it's adventure time." She looked Mack in the eye. "You okay with that? Nobody but you loves her more than those two. Think she'll be safe with them?"

Mack felt as if the weight of the world was being lifted off him as he shook his head yes. He turned to Lisa, "Will that be okay? You won't be upset if we do it this way?"

She didn't answer. She instead pointed a finger at Ben and gave him a slight nod of her head.

The conversation turned to other things for the rest of the evening. Only two people among them were mostly quiet. Mack and Dale. They were both relieved and satisfied with the decision. Not only would Lisa be safe with them, but Ben and Roy would be far better cover for her than either Mack or Dale would have been. Having them with her erased any and all questions about the what, where, or why of her activities. There was no way he could worry about what she wanted. Not even silently, inside his own head.

Mack didn't talk at all to her about what they were going to do until they got into bed together that night. "Are you sure, Lisa," he asked, "that you're okay with the way we're going to handle all this? You won't be thinking now, will you, that I care more about the bear than I do about you?"

"No, I won't. I never have doubts about how much you care. In fact, it seems like you sometimes care too much. Several times, you've said you were going to leave me because you thought you were in my way of being who I really wanted to be and of what or who I really loved. That's never been even close to true. I know I get screwed up in the head sometimes when it comes to you and me, but I've never ever wanted you to, as you say it, get out of my way. You are my way. I mostly wanted you with me down in the cities so you wouldn't get those feelings again."

"How can you sure I won't get them now?"

"That's easy. With Dale, there was always the chance that we could do something wrong. Wrong at least, for what we were supposed to be doing. I know that anything that happens between Dale and me has to be at the right time and place. If it isn't, you always get the wrong feelings about me. With Ben and Roy, there's no chance in hell you can get any of those feelings or ideas. They are the two most honorable men on this planet."

Mack pulled her close. "I'm sorry," he whispered in her ear. "I don't mean to get that way. It's just that you have had too much taken away from you. When those men did to you all the things they did to you, it tore me apart. You lost a lot. I just don't want to be someone in your life who will cause you to lose anything more. I love you too much. That's why I tell you I'll get out of your way. It seems like you always deserve more than what you get."

"No, Mack, I don't. I for the most part get more than I should. Especially the love I get from you. Add to that, you let me sometimes remind myself that I must be an okay person, no matter what those men did to me."

"That's your time with Dale, isn't it?"

"It is. As much as I care about and for him, I probably wouldn't ever do with him what I do, if it weren't for what was done to me then. They degraded me so bad that sometimes when I remember, I feel worthless. You always make me feel as though I'm worth a lot. Dale makes me feel as though that worth goes beyond love."

"I know. The thing is, when it happens you should let it be a thing of joy. You should take all the pleasure from it you can. I wouldn't want anything less for you."

"Is that what you do with Kathy, Mack?"

"It's what I try to do. I take as much from it as I can. Then I try to give even more back."

"I guess it's okay for me to tell you now. I try to do the same, Mack. It seems to me that to do it any other way would be wrong. If a person is going to do that, no matter the reason, it better mean something. If you don't truly feel it to your bones, don't do it."

Mack kissed her. "So, how do your bones feel when you're with me?"

"Like they're on fire and my body is going to explode. Like it's everything life is or could be. Sometimes I wonder if I'm going to ever return to any other part of life. I could live okay without Dale in my life. I'd just rather not. You, however, I'm not so sure. If I lost you, I'd probably stay alive. I just don't think I'd go on living."

"I feel the same way about you. Given we both feel that way, I think we should set our selves and this bed on fire now? Do you think we can accomplish that?"

"If we can't, then we aren't who we've always been. You don't know it, but when I was supposed to be too young, my fingers filled my dreams about the fires I wanted to light with you."

Mack moved over her. "You know how to use your fingers now, don't you?"

She gave a soft moan as she expertly used them to guide him where they both wanted him. With that they began to share what only could be shared together. Not any other way.

CHAPTER 14

Roy gave a lot of thought to Lisa's story about what she and Dale experienced the day they spent watching the football players at the mall. After all day there, they didn't accomplish anything until the night in the parking lot. He considered then what started the trouble that got Beth and Bob in the mess they were in.

It all happened in the mall's parking lot, not inside the mall. There were other kidnappings and rapes in parking lots and ramps he knew about too. Enough of them to make him think it would be a good idea to watch the one at this mall, rather than spend all their time inside it.

Ben and Lisa were sure the best way to accomplish what they were trying to do was to be as inconspicuous as possible. Roy had other ideas. He wanted the people, who thought they needed to somehow get rid of Beth and Bob, to notice them. He believed there would be a better chance of catching them making a mistake if they were spooked by knowing they were being watched.

"What I think will do more to get to those people is to make them wonder about us. They should think of us as strange, weird, and impossible to understand. We don't want them to see Ben and I the way they'd see Mack or Dale. We want them to look at us like we're hapless and helpless old men. People they can easily intimidate. We're going to damn sure dress the part too, which is to dress the way we normally do. I'm going to wear my western style clothes. Ben's going to wear his farmer overalls. And you, Lisa, are going to dress like a hillbilly. Whatever it is you wear should keep you decently covered. At the same time, whatever it is should be something that will make every man who sees you wish it didn't."

The next thing he insisted on doing to attract attention to them was to drive his truck. It was something that was noticed no matter where he drove it. The truck was a one ton Chevrolet with a stake cargo bed. Roy had completely restored it. It's dark green paint shined as bright as any new truck. The wheels were chrome and the tires were old-fashioned whitewalls. Inside the cab was a bench seat. The transmission was a standard and the gear shift was on the floor, which meant Lisa needed to be careful where she kept her legs.

Everything inside the cab carried the same shine as the paint on the outside. Nearly new rubber mats covered the floor. What made the truck as special as it was, was under the hood. A four hundred plus horse power V8 powered it. Every metal part on the engine or its peripherals was chrome and sparkling.

It was Roy's pride and joy, and stood out even when he showed it in antique car shows. In the mall everyone who came within eyesight of it noticed it. Most of the young people who did only thought of it as a nice old truck. Older people, some of whom were old enough to be alive when the truck was made, admired the work Roy put into it when he restored it.

Very little was going on when they first got to the mall, so they went inside for coffee. No one paid much attention to them until a group of men noticed Lisa. They were dressed in tight pants and loose shirts left halfway unbuttoned to show off their chests. Each of them had some kind of gold necklace on. None of the four were particularly big, but they all looked like they would know how to fight if it ever came to one.

Ben and Roy were aware of their stares and quiet comments, but ignored them as long as they could. From their dress and overall looks, Roy was fairly sure they were pimps taking a break after riding herd all night on the women they controlled.

He hoped the men would keep their interest in Lisa to stares and comments. He didn't want any trouble with them, knowing if there was any it could interfere with what they were there to do. They weren't going to be so lucky. One of the men approached their table.

He gave them his best and biggest smile. "How's you folks today?" he asked, bending down and resting his palms on the edge of their table.

"We are just fine," Roy answered, his tone telling the man he wasn't welcome where he was. "And we'll be a hell of a lot better when you get your hands the hell off our table."

The man quickly straightened up. He rubbed his hands together as if he picked up something unclean from the table. He kept his smile. "We been watching you folks," he said, trying to make his voice somewhat intimidating. "We been wondering, what the hell it is you old men is doin' with this here pretty young thing. It can't be good. You is way too old for you to be messing with her. We was thinking, it's goin' to be a good idea for her to come sit with us."

"Ain't going to happen," Roy growled back at him. "She's staying right where she is. So why don't you shuffle your pathetic pimps ass back to where you came from."

The look on the man's face made it obvious that he didn't like being called a pimp. "You know, it ain't what you'd call healthy to be calling people names. I don't take kindly to it at all."

Roy stood up and stared hard into his eyes. "I frankly don't give one rat's ass about how you take anything. Lisa is with us and she will be staying with us. She doesn't like pimps any better than I do. In fact, she hates each and everyone of you with a passion so deep she'd prefer to kill you, rather than let you continue to walk around. If you don't turn around and walk away now, I'm going to let her get up and do to you what I know she very much wants to do."

The man laughed at that. He was sure Roy was only running off at the mouth. There was no way, he was sure as most men were when they first saw Lisa, that she was as harmless as she was defenseless. There just was no way he was going to back up because of what Roy said about her.

That's when things changed. The three men still sitting at the own table were listening to their disagreement. When one of the three heard Roy mention Lisa by name, his eyes got as big a saucers. He shook his head, then waved at the man badgering Roy. The man ignored him.

The man at the table waved franticly for the pestering one to leave them and return to their table. It did no good, so the table man rushed over and asked Roy, "Is that young lady Lisa Thomas? I heard you say her name, and then tell my friend here you were going to let her do what she wants to do. If she is Lisa Thomas, then letting her get after him would be a terrible thing to do. I know he's a pain in the ass, but he don't deserve what she'd do. We'd be leaving now."

He took his friend by the arm and dragged him away. "If you'd of had to tangle with that woman," he told him, "you might well have ended up dead. If not, you'd sure be wishing you'd a minded your own business the way we told you you should, before you went over and bugged them folks. They ain't none of them nobody too fuck with. I seen her get pissed at one of us once. It ain't something what I'd ever want to see again."

The four men left their table, the cafeteria, and then the mall. Roy, Ben, and Lisa waited for a while before they went outside again. Ben, more than the other two, chuckled all the way out.

"Seems like you've got a good reputation among those people," he said to Lisa when they got into Roy's truck.

"I hope so," Lisa answered. "Everyone of them is on my special list. It's a list that will only get longer. What those men do does not now nor will it ever give me anything but bad thoughts about them. If everyone of them on the face of the earth died instantly, right now, I wouldn't have so much as a single tear to shed for them. They are, each and everyone, the filth and garbage of the human race. They are as bad as any of the worst of us, no matter what their crime."

"Even as bad as Trump?" Roy asked.

"Definitely. Trump's just another lowlife pimp. Always has been, always will be. The people who voted for him voted for the degradation of human life all over the entire planet. They were all just too stupid to know it."

"I sure can't argue on that."

"I can't either," Ben said. "But there's a couple of kids a couple of rows over waving at us. It looks like they want us to stop. I think we should. One of them is crying."

Roy stopped where he was so Ben and Lisa could check out the two boys right away. They ran through a couple of rows of cars as Roy drove around them. When they reached the boys, the crying one was standing there with a lost look on his face, staring into space almost as if he was blind. The second boy was kneeling down, gently petting a dog. A dog who appeared to be gravely injured.

"What happened?" Ben asked.

"Some high school boys ran over him. He wasn't hurting nobody or nothing. I think he was lost. Why'd they have to run him over?"

"He's not your dog?"

"No. He was just running loose. I think he must have run away. Or else maybe someone let him loose here."

Lisa kneeled down to check the dog. "She's still alive, Ben. We can't just leave her here."

"I know. Let's see what Roy says."

Roy agreed with Lisa. They couldn't just leave the dog lay there to die. Let's take her to a vet."

"In a minute," Ben said. "Do you know where the boys who did this went?" he asked the two boys.

"They parked and went in the mall. They were laughing. I guess they thought it was fun to run over a dog."

Ben's face was filled with anger. "You and Lisa take the dog and get her patched up, if she can be patched up," he told Roy and Lisa. "If not, they might have to put her down. Either way, we got to do what we can to help her."

"What are you going to do?" Roy asked.

"I'm going in the mall with these two boys. We are going to see if we can find the ones who did this. After that, I'm hoping I can wait for you to get back while I watch them. A little talk with them when you do might not hurt."

"And if they decide to leave before we get back."

"I guess I'll have to play it by ear. Either way, it'll be best if you get going. The sooner the dog gets to a vet the better."

Even though they were concerned about leaving Ben there alone, they knew that they needed to get the dog some help. So Lisa and Roy left with the dog. Lisa was busy searching for a vet on her GPS system.

Ben went into the mall with the two boys. They quickly found the three boys who were in the car that ran over the dog. It was immediately obvious that they felt zero remorse about what they'd done to the dog.

Ben gave each of the boys who saw the dog get run over five dollars and told them to leave. They did. He sat down to wait. As he watched, he didn't like at all what he saw. The boys were not nice people. The best one word description for them was, they were creeps.

He found it difficult to wait. What he wanted to do was get up and treat them to what they had coming. The only thing that kept him from doing what he wanted was their age. Two of the three looked under eighteen. The third one looked a couple of years older.

Ben was sure right away that he would probably end up losing sight of the boys if they decided to go out into the mall. He didn't plan on following them, because if he did, he'd have trouble connecting up with Roy and Lisa when they returned. Something he was sure would be quite a while. The visit to the vet was going to take too much time.

He was wrong though, about how long they'd both be gone. Roy returned in slightly less than an hour. Ben was glad to see him, but his first reaction was that the dog must be dead if he was back already.

"No," Roy explained, "the dog's still alive. As soon as we got into the vet's and told them what happened, I left Lisa there to deal with it and came back here. We didn't know what we'd left you to deal with exactly, so we agreed this would be the best thing to do. Lisa would have preferred to be the one who came back, but she didn't want to drive my truck. She said that since my truck was what my truck was, she didn't want to take a chance on driving it."

"I can't blame her for that, Roy. I wouldn't care to drive it either. That thought aside, what the hell do you think we should do about those boys? It sure as hell doesn't look like they give even one kind of a damn about what they did to the dog."

"It surely doesn't. Watching kids like those three makes me wonder about the future of this country of ours. At the same time, I know that it doesn't matter what generation it is or was, there's always some bad among the mostly okay kids. It doesn't seem like there's any place or anything happening without at least one bad person being part of it."

"It's too bad they aren't older, Roy. We could push them into a fight and then beat the living hell out of them."

"I agree. The trouble is, the world is full of disappointments. We can, however, have a little talk with them. It won't hurt the world any for them to hear what we think of them, will it?"

"Not so much I'd notice, no. Who knows, it might do the little bastards some good?"

"It might, Ben. I seriously doubt it, but I guess it might."

"Either way, I think you're right. A little talk with them is in order."

The boys were not happy to have two old men sit down at their table with them. The older of the three, Ralph Tomkins, said so. "There's lots of other tables," he complained, "so go sit at one of them. We damn sure don't want a couple of old homos sitting with us."

"The thing about that is," Ben answered, "we don't in any way care what it is that you do or don't want. You miserable brats ran over a dog intentionally, so we decided we'd tell you why you were so wrong when you did it."

"There was nothing wrong with doing it," Ralph claimed. "It was just a scraggly old stray. The best thing for it was to put it out of its misery."

"The thing is, you didn't. All you did was hurt it bad and make it even more miserable. You didn't even stop to check on it. What you did was pure mean and not one damn other thing. If I wouldn't go the jail for it, because you're so young, I'd take you outside and beat the crap out of you. Then I'd leave you lay there like what you did to the dog. Someone who, by the way, has probably a hundred times the value you and your two buddies combined have."

Ralph snickered. "It's like this old man, you couldn't in any way beat me. You can't possibly have enough left in you to do it. I'm too strong. I constantly train, so I'm always in good shape. I have to be. I'm a starting fullback for our team, so I have to be."

"You're a football player? For what team?"

Ralph told him.

"What about these two characters with you? They play too?"

"Not yet. They got one more season to wait before they're old enough to play with us. I'll be playing in college by then."

Ben looked at the two younger boys. "It's your plan then," he said to them, "to along with being dog killers, you're going to be rapists and murderers too? Those aren't exactly noble ambitions."

Both boys dropped their mouths open at Ben's accusations. They quickly gave each other a hard look, then one of them said, "I just want to play football. I don't want to do any of that other stuff. I was just in the car. I didn't run over the dog."

"If you don't want to do those other things, Boy," Roy asked him, "then what are you doing hanging out with trash like him?"

"He's helping me with my training. I'm a quarterback, and he's working with me. I'm lucky to have his help.'

"You might think so," Ben said. "I don't. Be my guess too, that all three of you think it was okay for that pissant quarterback of yours to attack and try to rape a couple of innocent women? One of whom was just told that morning that she had breast cancer. Then it was okay and near kill a man who was only trying to help them?"

"Oh my god," Ralph said. "You must be one of them strange people from up north. I want you to get the hell away from us right now, or else I'm going to call the police."

"We will be more than glad to leave you miserable things alone. First, I want you to hear this. I want you to tell everyone who plays on or is,.m connected to the loser football team you're part of that we are looking forward to tangling with all of you. If any of you so much as come into our county, you will regret it."

"I ain't telling nobody nothing."

"That's fine too. You know it and that's what matters most. When we get done with all of them, you can be glad you stayed home and away from what all of them are going to get from us. You being the small time little coward who you most definitely are."

"I'm not a coward. I play football. It takes guts to do that."

"If you say so, you being the brave one who intentionally runs over innocent dogs just for the hell of it. Coward is one of the milder words I could use to describe you." Roy turned to Ben. "Let's leave this trash now. I'm curious as to how the vet's doing with the dog anyway."

The boys were quiet as they watched Ben and Roy leave. Something strange was happening to them. They were asking themselves if they were really right when they all decided to run over the dog. They certainly didn't think anyone else would care about it. So why did those two old men from way up north care. Not only care, but care enough to take it to a vet. They were spending money on a dog that wasn't even theirs. Why would anyone do something like that? It was just a dog they were now going to go check on.

When Ben and Roy joined her, Lisa was sitting alone, waiting for word about the dog. The vet's office staff had chosen to pretty much ignore her. They'd thought of her and Roy as a bit strange when they brought the dog in. Their dress was unusual for that part of the world, as was their reason for bringing the dog there. People bringing stray dogs that had just been run over by what they claimed was some kids, were something else that was close to never seen either.

And the truth of it was, they would have refused to even look at the dog if Lisa hadn't been willing to let them hold one of her credit cards. A card they checked to be sure it would cover the exorbitant fees they planned to charge her for what they did. Fee's that would be equally high whether the dog lived or died.

It was another hour of waiting before the vet finally saw them. "The dog is still alive," he said, "but she's going to need to be hospitalized for a few days. Even then, I wouldn't give her chances of survival more than about fifty-fifty. I have to tell you, her care will get expensive. The best thing for you and her will probably to put her down."

"It looks like you already put a lot of effort to help her," Lisa said. "Why do that if you think putting her down is the best thing to do?"

"It was an emergency when I started working on her, and I didn't know who you folks were. Now that I do, it appears that the amount of money it could cost to keep the dog alive, in hopes it'll get better, might place an unnecessary burden on you. Especially since she isn't even your dog."

"I guess that depends on how you look at it. Do you have the facilities here to take care of the dog?"

"We do. I have to say this again though. It will be expensive. Are you sure you want to do this?"

"I am," Lisa said without the slightest hesitation. The only thing expensive meant was that part of the money Mack always felt so uncomfortable about having would go to a worthy cause. And, if she didn't tell the vet to do what he could for the dog, Mack would be upset with her. For him, there would never be any other choice. "You have my credit card information. You can call me when the dog is either well enough to leave here, or if she doesn't make it. Either way, I expect you to do everything you can for her. You don't have to ask me about each step you take or administer any needed drugs. Just do your best."

"Okay. I guess it's your money. It's not up to me to tell you how to spend it."

With that, Lisa, Ben, and Roy left the vet's office. It was after lunchtime by then so they decided to get something to eat. They found a local bar that according to the reviews they found online served good burgers and ate there.

When they finished what proved to be a decent meal, they went back to the mall to again do some patrolling. It didn't take long for them to pick out the various people watching them. Some were in cars and others were on foot, but they all were looking for trouble.

It was exactly what Roy, Ben, and Lisa were expecting.

CHAPTER 15

Julie Anderson decided to take a long lunch and use the time to visit her father, Bob Anderson at the rehabilitation center. She normally went to see him and her step mother, Beth, in the evening. She missed doing it the previous evening because she had a date with her new love interest, Lenard Schultz, the man who was now Beth's body guard. They'd managed the date because a man who was part of the US Marshall service with Lenard stayed with Beth for the few hours they were out.

Lenard was, of course, happy to see her when she arrived at the facility. She was equally glad to see him. Even so, they were careful to hold back the show of the affection they had for each other to a mild hug. Bob was awake, and they didn't want to do anything that had even the slightest chance of upsetting him. The realization of how much his youngest daughter had grown up might do that. Especially now that his physical condition was making him feel older than he was.

Julie then spent the rest of her time talking with her father. Beth used her visit as a chance to step outside to get a fresh breath and take a short walk. The courtyard at the back of the center was nothing fancy. The best thing about it was simply the fact that it was outside, and it took Beth out of the stifling environment found in nearly all medical facilities, regardless of their purpose. She still managed to take full advantage of it in the short time she was able to be out there. She walked the narrow paths and did enjoy the few blossoms in the flowers still blooming.

When it was time for Julie to go back to work, she met with Beth outside in the courtyard. Lenard, who was staying close to Beth up until then, backed off some in order to give them some privacy as they said their goodbyes for the day.

What none of them noticed was the apparently older woman, who was actually not at all old, who was using a walker, enter the courtyard from the street behind them. She was moving at an almost impossible slow pace as she seemed to be searching for something in her oversized purse, which was in the basket at the front of the walker.

What the old woman was reaching for was her recently purchased hand gun. She was able to buy it without any background checks or waiting, because she purchased it from a private dealer at a gun show.

The only thing holding her back from pulling the gun out was Lenard. He was standing between her and the two women. He was, until recent months, her fiancé, and she was still in love with him. That's why she was there. Shiela James was sure Beth was trying to steal Lenard away from her. And now things were even worse for her. The way Lenard acted when he was near the beautiful young women talking to the evil Beth didn't seem right. She was sure as soon as she saw Julie, that she would need to shoot her too.

The problem was, she didn't dare shoot yet. She knew she wasn't proficient enough with her gun to totally trust her accuracy. With Lenard standing where he was, there was a chance she might hit him, however slim it might be. Since her reason for being there was mainly to get him back, she certainly didn't want to shoot him.

Shiela was now in a bad position. If she continued walking the path she was on, it would wind around to the point it would bring her close enough to Lenard for him to recognize her. She didn't want him to do that. If he did, he would expect her to tell him why she was there. She certainly couldn't tell him. He might not love her again if he knew she was there to kill the two women there trying to steal him from her.

What she'd forgotten, after she convinced herself he would want her back, was that the major reason he'd broken up with her was because of her constant, but unjustified, jealousy. It had gotten to the point that their relationship was completely dysfunctional.

Shiela herself was for the most part dysfunctional. Her mental condition was at the point where she needed serious treatment. Her psychiatrist had already prescribed some serious antidepressant drugs for her, but she'd failed to take them.

Even if she had, she was delusional enough to be where she was. She couldn't find a way to acknowledge the truth. Lenard was no longer in love with her, and even if he was, there was little he could do to help her. She was at the point where only professional help could save her.

Nothing like that concerned her now. She was too convinced that all of the problems she and Lenard had were the fault of other women. Especially the two women he was with in this courtyard.

Tired of waiting for the three people she was watching to get in the right positions, she decided she would shoot the women where they were. The one thing Shiela forgot about doing while she was trying to decide when to start shooting, was what Julie was doing during that time. Which was constantly watching everything around her.

All the training she'd gone through and was still going through to be a private detective was now about to pay off. When Shiela made her decision and pulled out her gun, the sudden movement caught Julie's eye. She pushed Beth away as hard as she could, then dropped down on the ground. She had her own gun out even before she landed. Unfortunately, Shiela managed to fire two shots before Julie hit her in the chest with two of her own.

One of Shiela's bullets hit Lenard on the left part of his back. It missed his heart, but left a mess when it exited his chest. The bullets from Julie's gun that hit Shiela in the chest did the job. She was dead.

Beth screamed and put both hands over her face. She couldn't believe what she'd just seen. Two people were on the ground in front of her, with both of them in pools of blood. How could this have happened, and more than that, how could this child she helped raise manage to save her life and shoot someone too.

Julie was shaken, but far better prepared to deal with it mentally than Beth. She immediately called 911. In minutes, they could hear the sirens on the way. She then called Dale. He answered his personal cell phone, then told her he was already on the way.

The ambulance was the first to arrive on the scene. It had made a delivery to the hospital and was just leaving it when the call came through. So it was only a couple of blocks away at the time. A sheriff's deputy was only seconds behind it. She ignored the ambulance people to start, and joined Julie and Beth to question them. Before she could ask a question, Dale got there.

He shook his head in disbelief when he saw the bodies. "What happened, Julie?" he asked her. "Did you shoot both of them?" He pointed at the bodies on the ground. One being worked on by a paramedic and the other obviously dead.

"No. She shot Lenard. I shot her. I don't know who she is. I just know she took out a gun. She fired before I did, that's why Lenard got shot."

"It took Julie longer to shoot, Dale," Beth managed to choke out, "because she pushed me out of the way first. I'm not sure who that person on the ground wanted to shoot, but I think it was me. Julie saved my life."

"I'm not surprised. She's like her sister. Putting the other person first."

"And I'll be forever grateful," Beth said. "But can I go check on Bob. I'm sure he's real scared now that something might have happened to us."

"Yes, go ahead," Dale agreed. "I might have more questions, but they can wait. Bob's more important."

Dale paused a moment to call Mack. Julie was already on the phone with Lisa, who said they were on their way home as soon as Julie told her what happened. Only Roy knew right away that there were three carloads of men of various ages following them as they left the mall parking lot.

Mack's answer for Dale was with a voice filled with urgency. "I was just about to call you, Dale," he said. "I've got a bunch of assholes here with guns pointed at me. They said they were looking for the bear. I guess they need to kill it real bad. They are definitely filled with a blood lust. Since there's no way I'm going to let them do it, I could use your help."

"To start, Mack, I'll have to send a couple of deputies. I've got a situation here at the rehabilitation center. Someone was here, apparently hoping to shoot Beth. Whoever the person was, she's dead. Julie was here and took her out. Lenard was shot. I'll get back to you when I know more."

When Beth went back inside the center, it was mostly filled with confusion. Everyone there was now aware that there was a shooting, but for the most part didn't know any of what actually happened. The staff of the place was just scared, and to a large extent ignored any of the needs patients might have because of the shooting.

Going into Bob's room, Beth found herself facing another disaster. The panic everyone was showing around Bob was having a strong negative effect on him. His already disease weakened heart was now showing signs of stress. Its irregular beat was weak and his breathing was shallow. It was obvious that he needed immediate medical attention. She called 911, hoping to get an ambulance for him right away. He needed to be in a hospital. She was told they would get one to him, but the only one available was out of town. It was going to take it a while for it to get there.

Beth went out to see if Dale could help her with Bob. Julie went into Bob's room with Dale and Beth. She knew the second she saw her father that he couldn't wait for the ambulance. He needed help now.

Dale agreed with her. He went out in the main lobby of the place and captured a large male nurse trying to figure out what to do next. He and Dale managed to get Bob out of his room and into the backseat of Dale's car. Beth rode in the front seat. Julie followed in her own car, terrified that she might lose her father and her lover at anytime. The emergency staff was waiting when Dale pulled up to the emergency entrance. But even seeing them didn't ease Julie's stress much.

Bob was quickly moved to a gurney and rolled inside the hospital. The first doctor next to him with a stethoscope shook his head. He didn't like what he heard inside Bob's chest.

As they wheeled him into the critical care unit, Beth, Julie, and Dale were told to wait in the lobby. Julie again called Lisa to tell her what was going on.

"I'm sorry, Julie," she answered, "but I really can't talk right now. We've got three cars on our tail and the people inside them aren't at all happy with us. I need to call Dale."

"Okay, Lisa, but Dale's right here. Hang on." She handed her phone to Dale.

He listen for about a minute, then turned his back on Julie and Beth and walked far enough away so they couldn't hear what he was telling Lisa. It didn't help any. They knew, just by his movement, that something was seriously wrong there too.

That's when Dale's phone rang. He tried to answer it while still staying connected with Lisa on Julie's phone. He would have ignored his own phone, but the special ring told him it was Mack. And he knew Mack was in trouble too.

Julie knew from what she was watching that there was trouble on the other end of both conversations Dale was having. She took her phone back from Dale. "What is it you need us to do, Lisa?"

"Get ready to stop these guys behind us," she said, sounding as if she was out of breath, when she was just very excited. She knew that if they could trap this bunch chasing them now, it would go a long way toward putting a stop to their vendetta against Beth, Bob and all the rest of them.

"We'll all do the best we can," Julie promised. "But there's a lot going on right now. Mack's got some kind of problem at the refuge too. He's asking for help."

"Do what you can," Lisa said, then suddenly they were disconnected.

At the same time, Dale heard a gunshot from Mack's phone. Things went silent for him too. He did the only thing he could do to get things moving as fast as possible. He called the dispatcher and told her to get on the radio and send every car available to the wildlife refuge. Today it was as important as it had ever been in the past, to keep Mack alive. Losing either him or Lisa would be devastating. Losing both of them was impossible to comprehend.

Julie told Dale more about the trouble Lisa was in, and he got busy trying to set up something to assist her and Ben and Roy as much as possible. Julie was doing the same thing with everyone from Refuge Rescuers. As much as she was worried about Bob and Lenard, she knew she didn't have a choice.

As much as Julie was concerned about her father, and how Beth was going to react if the worst happened, she knew she had to give Lisa first priority. So she left when Dale did. All she could do about her father and Lenard, who was being operated on, was hope.

In truth, she need a lot of that for Lisa, Ben, and Roy. Not to mention Mack and Shanty, who were in grave danger at the refuge.

CHAPTER 16

It was a standoff. Mack and Shanty against a dozen men armed with high powered rifles. The men wanted to know where the bear was. They were there to kill the dangerous creature. For them they said, it was the only choice. It was way too dangerous for their children to allow it to continue to roam the refuge.

Fred Nicholes was the leader of the bunch. He was the father of Teddy Nicholes, who was one of the kids doing volunteer work at the refuge. Fred hated the refuge because his rundown farm was one of the land acquisitions Mack and Shanty made during the expansion phase of the restoration of the refuge. He was sure that he should have been paid more for his farm than he was. It didn't mean anything to him that he was paid several thousand dollars over the market value for the farm. Nor did the fact that he was desperate for the money when he sold it.

He decided he should have gotten more money because he spent what he got on night life or lost the rest of it at the casino. When Mack and Shanty decided to use high school kids, who were interested in the refuge, as volunteer workers, Fred pushed Teddy to join up. He wanted him there to spy on the project, and to make as much trouble for Mack and Shanty as he could.

Mack was quickly aware that Teddy wold be mostly trouble within minutes of his arrival with the other volunteer kids. His first reaction was to send him back to town on the bus that brought them all to the refuge. But Mack saw something in the kid that said he should give him a chance.

With Mack's patience and guidance, Teddy was beginning to not only understand what the refuge was about, but to appreciate the experience he was getting by being allowed to work there. That was something that infuriated Fred, and had as much to do with wanting to kill the bear as anything.

He knew enough about Mack's reputation to know that Mack was very protective of all the animals who were part of the refuge, which made killing the bear a good way to get some revenge. The other big reason for killing the bear was the joy of the killing itself. It would be a real thrill to kill a large, dangerous animal. And that's the main reason the other men were with him. For the chance to shoot and kill a bear.

They were upset too, because they were true believers in capitalism. The latest and loudest teachings of the various evangelical churches they belonged to. Socialism was against God's will, they were told, and wildlife refuges, along with parks, were pure socialism. Never mind that this one was totally privately owned. It was open to the public for various recreational activities free of charge. Socialism at its worst.

The problem the macho men were having was finding the bear. They were demanding that Mack tell them where to find it. It never occurred to them that the bear was a large enough animal to wander over many miles on any given day. That meant that even if Mack was willing to tell them anything about the bear's location, he couldn't.

"I can't tell you where the bear is," Mack explained, "because I don't have any idea where it is. Where she goes and what she does is not something she tells me. I guess she considers it her own business. And the truth is, so do I. You are all wasting your time with this. Why don't you get smart and get the hell out of here before we call the sheriff and have you all arrest for trespassing and bringing a gun into this refuge."

Fred shrugged and rolled his shoulders, trying to make himself look as big as possible. "This is supposed to be open to the public. So you can't claim we're trespassing. The second amendment to the constitution says we get to carry guns, so you can't do nothing about that either. We have the right to defend ourselves, so unless you tell us where that bear is, a couple of us will be defending ourselves against you."

That was enough of a threat to tell Shanty that it was a good idea to call the sheriff's office. She used Mack's phone to call Dale. She knew that Dale had his phone set up so it rang special if Mack or Lisa called him. At the same time Dale answered, a shot rang out. She looked up to see Teddy sink down to his knees. A red splotch on his chest was growing larger.

Shanty charged Fred. He'd just shot his own son. She grabbed his rifle by the barrel and ripped it out of his hands. Holding the rifle by the barrel with both hands, she swung it with everything she had. The butt of the gun slammed onto the side of Fred's head. He fell to the ground unconscious. He had a skull fracture.

Suddenly then, the bear came crashing out of some nearby brush. She rushed to Teddy and stood over his body to protect it. None of the men who came to the refuge with Fred cared one way or the other what it was that she was doing. She was a big bad bear and a perfect target. All of the men lifted their guns to shoot her. Before they could fire, a second bear charged them. She was followed by four half grown cubs. The five of them lit into the, anxious to kill something, men. Only one of them managed to do anything. He shot one of the cubs.

Mack lost it then. He grabbed a rifle from the closet man and started swinging it. Three men went down before he needed to stop the swing and reverse the direction of the flying rifle. When he did, there was nothing close enough to him to hit. The new bear and her uninjured cubs were busy with the want-to-be killers.

Shanty finished the phone call to Dale and picked up the twelve gauge, pump shotgun she always kept close. She fired the first shot in the air. "All of you, drop your guns or I damn well will turn this shotgun on you. There are enough shells in it to take everyone of you useless bastards out, which I'd love to do, so go ahead and give me an excuse."

Mack dropped the rifle and went to Teddy, hopping he was wrong and there would be something he could do. There was. The bear moved out of Mack's way so he could check on Teddy. He was alive, and Mack immediately did everything he could to stop the bleeding. Shanty patched up the wound in the bear cubs shoulder and watched idiot macho men until the sheriff's deputies got there. By the time they did, the ambulance for Teddy was almost there, and all the bears, including the injured cub, were long gone.

With his anger at the edge, Mack would have liked to do a lot more to the mighty child and bear shooters, but knew he would be the one to pay for it if he did. To avoid dwelling on what was done by the stupidity of the men who had come there to fulfill a bloodlust, Mack started questioning the men. He hoped to piece together what happened to Teddy.

Most of the men wouldn't talk at all. It wasn't until he started questioning a younger man, who said he was Teddy's cousin, that Mack got some answers.

"I was standing next to Fred," he explained. "He actually did kind of a jump, he got so excited all the sudden. He pointed at some bushes and yelled, 'the bear' and moved his gun up to shoot it. That's when Teddy surprised all of us. He jumped in front of Fred so he couldn't shoot that damn bear. Why'd he do that? It was just a bear. They ain't really worth nothing. It don't make no sense, him getting shot to save a bear."

Shanty, who felt some sympathy for the man said, "I think it was because in the short time he worked with us, he was learning to respect all life forms. He knew the bear was something special. He knew she wasn't dangerous. Most of all, he knew his idiot father was wrong to want to shoot it."

"Well, that's stupid. All human life is sacred. Everyone knows that. Them other things what live in this refuge don't matter a damn. He shouldn't of done that."

"No," Mack said, "Fred shouldn't have been so overly anxious to kill something. If he had a functioning brain, he would have listened to me and left the bear alone."

"I don't know about that. That bear was a killer. You seen the way she come out a them bushes to attack Teddy when he was shot."

"You are an idiot, the same as Fred," Mack snapped at him. "You are stupid beyond stupid. What the bear did when she moved over Teddy the way she did, was to protect him. She knew he was hurt. All of you useless assholes are lucky. If she wouldn't have tried to protect him, she'd have ripped a lot more of you to shreds. I'm sorry now that she didn't."

"That's a hell of a thing to say."

"Not really. That bear was worth more than any hundred people like you or any of the rest of these killers here."

"Speaking of them," he asked, "shouldn't we be helping the ones what are bleeding?"

"Go ahead. You're one of them. Give them all the help you want to. From my point of view, there ain't a damn one of them worth the effort."

Mack looked around then, at the ground littered with guns. He picked them up, one at a time and smashed their stocks over a large rock when he could. The rest he did his best to destroy however he could. They looked like a pile of rubble when the sheriff's deputies arrived.

Mack was surprised when only two of them came. When he asked about Dale, he was told about Lisa, Ben, and Roy, and how most of the rest of the sheriff's department was out on the four lane, hoping to stop the three carloads of men from the cities chasing them.

Mack sat down on a tree stump then, terrified about Lisa. It was all too much for him. He knew his ability to function was lost until he saw her safe and whole again. If he didn't, he wasn't sure he would survive the loss. The thought of losing Lisa, not to mention Ben and Roy, was overwhelming.

He broke out in a cold sweat and started to shake. Shanty was watching him, and quickly sat next to him when his trembling became severe. She put her arms around him and held him until it stopped and he was breathing normal again.

As it did, he turned to her, kissed her, and said, "Thank you."

She kissed him then, all the time hoping he wouldn't notice her tears.

CHAPTER 17

Roy was both thankful and proud of what his truck could do. He managed to consistently stay ahead of the three vehicles chasing them. And he was getting close enough to the Clayborne County line to be confident they would be able to turn things around.

That, however, depended on what Dale was able to put together for their rescue. Roy was sure it would take several sheriff's cars to trap all of the three behind him. They would likely need plenty of fire power too. He was sure that the people behind him were well armed, and more than ready to start shooting.

Dale, who was concerned that the few deputies he would be able to put together in the short time he had, would not be enough to contain all the people chasing Lisa, Roy, and Ben. As he struggled to find something more to use, other than sheriff's cars with flashing lights, to stop and hold the vehicles doing the chasing, he remembered the construction going on in a stretch of ditches next to the four lane about three miles inside the Clayborne County line.

There were several pieces of heavy equipment being used on the ditch rebuilding project. They could, Dale knew, provide a more than sufficient blockade to stop and hold the three chase vehicles. He was also sure that it would take more than a phone call to convince the construction foreman to assist the sheriff's department in apprehending the people so anxious to gain revenge for their injured quarterback.

Even though Dale pushed his car to its top speed to reach the construction site as quickly as possible, he still only had minutes to prepare for the coming conflict. He hit it lucky this time. The construction company doing the work was local, and the foreman of the crew there knew Dale well enough to accept his explanation of the problem.

Construction was immediately stopped. Two caterpillars were moved onto the northbound lane of the highway, their blades facing the oncoming traffic. Initially, they were set far enough apart to let one lane of traffic through. The men who operated the machines stayed with them and kept them running so they were set to close the highway when the chase cars reached them.

To ensure that the chase cars and the people inside them couldn't find another escape route, other construction equipment was lined up along the sides of the highway. Four sheriff's cars were poised to move onto the highway behind the chase cars once they were stopped.

As they prepared the construction site for the capture, Dale talked to Roy over his cell phone, explaining to him what the plan was. Roy thought it was a good one, but knew that if it was going to work the way they wanted it to, he was going to have to let the chase cars get closer.

As soon as he backed off on the speed some, the men chasing him were thrilled. They were sure now that they were going to catch the trouble makers they were chasing. They knew that the bitch woman, Lisa Thomas, was in the truck. She was the one they wanted most. She destroyed their chance of a championship football season when she attacked and crippled their star quarterback for something as trivial as a disagreement about sex. His giving them the championship was certainly a lot more important than whether she wanted it or not. It was her place to take it, like it or not. Especially when a star quarterback was involved.

The men in the lead chase car who were sitting next to a window, decided it was time to slow Roy's truck down even more. They started shooting, thinking they could take out the rear tires. The truck had duel wheels in the back. The would be shooters were wildly off the mark with their hand guns.

For the most part, they were lousy shots even when they were in a stationary position on solid ground. Shooting from a speeding vehicle with their arms out a window, left them little chance of hitting their chosen targets. After firing close to fifty rounds, they finally took out one rear tire on Roy's truck. Not enough to stop him.

They did manage to hit a couple of mail boxes and and a dairy farmer's best milking cow, who was standing next to a fence built too close to the highway. It was just enough shooting to totally justify the trap Dale had waiting for them.

Roy's now flat, and already coming loose from its wheel, tire was flapping wildly as he sped between the two caterpillars waiting to block the highway. They started closing the gap in their blockade the instant he was through it.

The driver of the lead chase car was so excited about catching up with Roy, that he failed to see the trap he'd driven into. When he did realize it, he was too late to stop. The only option he had to avoid hitting a caterpillar blade head on was to put his car in a sideways slide. That's the way they slammed into the blade. It was enough to keep the crash from being fatal, but it did leave all six men in the car with serious injuries.

The next chase car slid sideways into the first car, leaving four of the the six men in that car with less serious injuries. The two men riding in the front seat were less lucky. Neither one of them was wearing a seatbelt. The men in the third car were all seriously injured. None of them were wearing seatbelts. When their car hit the first two head on, the two passengers in front were thrown through the windshield. They landed In the wreckage they hit. The rest of them were thrown around in their car.

It took four ambulances, who were called from a Minneapolis location, several trips to haul all eighteen of the men to the local hospital. From there, the worst of the injured men were flown to a trauma center in a large suburban hospital complex. The local hospital didn't have the facilities to handle that many serious trauma cases. Dale spoke to the chief of police of the suburb, and was told that the men would be held under arrest when they were healed enough to leave the hospital. They weren't.

Roy, Ben, and Lisa were relieved and grateful too Dale for doing such a good job handling their situation. The only people injured were the chasers. Lisa was especially pleased with Dale and the plan he came up with to rescue them. She felt then as though she must owe him something for doing it. Those feelings dominated her to the point she didn't listen very close when she was told that Mack and Shanty had gone through some serious trauma themselves at the refuge.

When she learned about what her sister Julie had been forced to do, she was taken even further away from any concerns she might have had about Mack or Shanty. Mack had no problem with that. Julie did need her sister to tell her it would all be okay. After, Julie decided to stay with Beth for the night. That way she would be closer to Lenard too. No matter what happened with him, she wanted to be close by when it did.

When Mack finally managed to get to the sheriff's office where everyone was by then, Lisa wasn't as receptive to Mack as he thought she would be. Even after all he and Shanty had gone through, his concern for her had been the most difficult for him to handle. The terror he'd felt over the thought that she, along with Ben and Roy, could be killed was still hanging over him.

He wanted to take her home with him right away, but Dale needed to keep her there as they finished up the investigation of what happened. Mack understood what needed to be done, but still felt a profound sense of something missing when he and Shanty left for home. He knew that everyone had things that were required to be done, but his time with Lisa left him with an uneasy feeling.

Shanty could tell that he was feeling off and probably a little lost. She could see the disappointment and concern in his face when Lisa was less receptive to him than she should have been.

Shanty wanted then, to tell Lisa what happened to them in the refuge, but held back. If Mack didn't tell her right away, she didn't think it was her place to do so either.

When they got home, she left him long enough to go to her house and take a shower. She needed to do something to get at least some of the feeling of the filth of the men who attacked them off her skin.

She thought about putting on a shirt and pants when she left the shower, but decided to wear something nicer. She put on a soft cotton blouse, which without the bra she decided to not wear, rested nicely on her body. The skirt she put on went perfectly with it. It was loose fitting, but just short enough so that if she wanted to, it was possible for her to let someone see that she didn't bother with panties either. She hoped it would be Mack looking.

She didn't plan to seduce Mack, but felt that it would be good for him if she could distract him from his gloomy thoughts. He was sitting on the rocking love seat when she joined him on his deck. She sat next to him, then took his hand and held it.

He lifted his sad eyes to her, nodded his head, then gave her a small smile as he squeezed her hand. They were quiet until Lisa finally got home. Mack left the love seat, walked to Lisa, and wrapped his arms around her. This time she sensed his need and hugged him back. She responded close to the way he hoped she would when he kissed her.

"I'm glad to see you too, Mack," she said. "But please, let me take a shower. I need to get the stink of this horrible day off me."

Mack did, but when he sat down again it was on a chair, separate from Shanty. She noticed it. It hurt. He was wrong when he didn't realize what he'd done by avoiding her. He wasn't the only one who needed some kind of comforting. A lot would happen before he would fully realize how he, as much as anyone, could ignore the needs of someone who deeply loved him.

When he did, the terror, the strangeness, and the beauty of it would leave him in a state of wondering.

CHAPTER 18

They were on Mack and Lisa's deck, and starting to relax with a beer. Lisa was exactly where Mack wanted her most. Snuggled in his lap. It was the one thing he needed that night. To be close to Lisa. He was finally getting to the point where he could tell her about the day from hell he and Shanty had. He was just waiting to get her full attention to do it. Something that wasn't quite there yet.

Dale was still at the office. Kathy was talking to him on the phone, and was just finishing the conversation with him. When she was done she told everyone about how stressed out and tired he was and about the paper work he was trying to finish up.

"If it's okay with you, Mack," Lisa suddenly said, thinking that this was a good way to repay what she thought she owed him for what he did that day, "I'm going to go into town and help him finish. It's all because of what happened with us today, so I think I should help him with it. He shouldn't have to be there, doing all that stuff alone. He should be sitting here with us."

"I don't know where that came from, but no, it's not," Mack answered her.

"What? What do you mean, it's not? Are you telling me you won't let me go help him?"

"Not at all. What I'm telling you is that it's not okay with me if you go."

"What's your problem with my doing it?"

"After all we've gone through today, I'd really appreciate having you here with me. I spent a lot of time afraid I might lose you today. You could have been killed. So now I need you to be here tonight. Not running into town for Dale. He can take care of the paperwork. He doesn't need you to help him with it. Or, if he's really that tired, he can finish it in the morning. He should be here with all of us anyway, not you going to him. If it mattered to him, he would be. So it's not okay with me if you go. I went through enough at the refuge already today. I don't want to lose you too Dale now. Expecting me too is expecting too much."

"You aren't losing me, but you are telling me I shouldn't go anyway. You've always said you wouldn't do that to me."

"I'm not telling you what you should or shouldn't do, Lisa. You asked me if it was okay with me if you went to town to help Dale. I just told you that it is not okay with me for you do. That's all I'm telling you. I'm not telling you that you can't go. I won't do anything to stop you if you decide you are going. I never get in the way of whatever it is that you want. It's just that tonight, I very much need and want you here. If you prefer to be with Dale rather than me, I sure as hell won't get in your way. I've told you many times I wouldn't get in the way of what you want. The choice whether or not you go is yours."

"I don't like the sound of that, Mack. What are you not saying? What's so important about tonight?"

"Everything there is about you and I and how much you mean to me. I already went through the terror of thinking I might lose you earlier. I don't want to do it again. And maybe I think I went through enough today. So if it is more important to go help Dale than staying here with me, you should take an overnight suitcase with you. I can't think of any other reason you going could be so important. I'd leave the house for you tonight, but I'm just too damn tired and beaten down right now to leave. I'll be gone by noon tomorrow. I won't be in your way again after that."

Shanty and Kathy had been careful to stay out of their disagreement, but Mack's answer shocked them. Still, they didn't say anything.

"So, you're telling me that if I go help him, I'm not coming home tonight? That you are leaving me? That's not what I'm going to do. I won't even be gone long. A couple of hours maybe. I just want to help a friend finish up what he's doing so he can come and be here with us. Why is that bothering you?"

Kathy, who was the most surprised by Mack's response to Lisa, now asked him the same question. "I want to know too, Mack. Why is her going to help Dale bothering you so much? She's helped him before."

"Because there's more to it than than her going to *help* him. She's putting Dale first in her life without thinking about what that means to me or anyone else right now. I guess I can understand why. He is a special person. But I'm her husband, and now she's made me second in her life. After all that happened today, the only thing I wanted tonight was to be close to her. I need for her to be here with me. There's only one reason for her to go running off to see Dale tonight, and I doubt like hell it's paperwork." He turned his focus from Kathy to Lisa. "I can't have this kind of relationship with you, Lisa. I care too much, I love you too much for it to be okay with me for you go. That doesn't mean you can't go to to see him when I need you here. You do what you want to do, what you think you need to do. As I've told you all along, I'll never tell you that you can't do what you think you need to do or want to do. Nor will I get in your way. Not even if it's only because you just want to. Again, I won't get in your way. But if you do go, be honest about why and take a suitcase with you. You'll want the right clothes for tonight and tomorrow."

There were some heads shaking now. What started as a disagreement and was now an argument which was so unexpected that it was leaving all of them stunned.

"That's not what I want to do. It's just a matter of helping a friend get some work done. After all he did for us today, I think I owe him that much."

"I suppose you do. The problem for me is, when you leave to go do whatever it is you are going to do with Dale, it will be over for you and I. I told you that I needed you with me tonight. It really matters to me that you being with Dale is more important to you than that. It shows me once more, that I really am in the way of what you want. Even if you realize what it means to me and come home before you get there, it will be over for us if you leave. You will already have thrown away much of what we've always had and have been. After all this time we've been together, you should understand how I feel right now. I can't live some kind of double life with you, and that's what you're making this. So I will be getting the hell out of your way, and out of your life. What you are doing now is exactly what just a couple of days ago you said you were so concerned about doing. That you absolutely didn't want to do. Apparently that wasn't true, and you don't have any real concern about it."

Lisa's mouth dropped open in disbelief. The shock of his words was enough to silence her.

Again, it was Kathy who spoke up. She very much needed him in her life. "Please, Mack, no matter what else you and Lisa might do, don't leave the rest of us. Shanty and I need you." She turned to Lisa. "You should think real hard about what you're doing. Helping Dale with some *goddamn* paperwork just *ain't* that *goddamn* important. You of all people should know that. It can always be done tomorrow." As she said it, she was beginning to think that it wouldn't be all bad if Lisa went. As much as she loved Dale, having Mack for the night or forever was something she would readily accept. Or even desire.

"But Mack's making me feel like he thinks I'm doing something wrong by just wanting to help a friend. A friend who saved my life today."

Mack told her. "After that bullshit comment, it sounds like you are not just determined to go, but desperate to go. So you might as well go and do your thing. It's always right to be independent. And right now, showing me that you are, and getting your way, is apparently more important than your marriage. So I think it's time to stop arguing. Go get yourself packed and ready and go see Dale."

"None of us can tell either one of you what to do," Kathy argued, "but you should stop and think about what you will both lose if you don't. Especially you, Lisa. I know Mack well enough to know that if you go too Dale tonight, he will leave you. If he does, I'm going with him. Then you will have Dale all to yourself."

"What do you all expect me to do?" Lisa asked. "I feel like I'll be doing the wrong thing now, no matter what I do."

"No, Lisa," Mack said. "The right thing for you to do is simple. Decide what matters the most and do it. You go, and you have Dale. That tells me he is what you want most. Something I knew as soon as you said you wanted to go to town to help him with his *paperwork*. As bad as you seem to want to go, I don't see that anything I say or do will matter. If you stay, maybe we can try to work past this. That is, if you want to? I'm not at all sure you do. The fact that you want to go even after I told you I need you to be with me tonight says it all. So again, let's stop fighting and get this over with. Go pack and get yourself ready. I have no doubts that Dale will be more than happy to see you."

"I'm going to call him now," Kathy said, "so he knows where

things are at. If he decides Lisa should go there and help him, he won't be welcome home tonight. And in that case, you're right, Lisa should take a suitcase. Or maybe a few of them. Make her time with him permanent. Mack and I will figure out what to do with our lives after the two of you are gone, Lisa."

"That's crazy. I don't want that. I'm sorry, Mack," Lisa said, wishing now that she'd have thought before she impulsively decided to go help Dale. "This wasn't at all because I want Dale more than you. It wasn't to start with. I just thought that it would be a nice thing to do to help him finish up his work tonight so he could spend the evening with us. I wanted to be the one to do that, because I'm the one who knows how to do the work. I just don't understand why you feel the way you do about it. That's why I've been arguing with you."

"You asked me, to start with, if it was okay with me for you go to town to spend the evening with Dale. I simply answered your question. It wasn't okay and I said it wasn't. You are the one who got upset. Not me. It still very much isn't okay with me. That doesn't mean I'm trying to tell you what to do. I didn't say you couldn't go. I only answered your question. Would it be okay with me? It's not. That said, all I've ever wanted is for you to be happy. I've always wanted more than anything, for you to be happy. It's just that there are things like what you want to do tonight that might make you happy that don't work for me. The reason I pulled you onto my lap when we sat down is because I so very much needed you there. I went through hell worrying about you when you guys were in trouble out on the highway. So now I don't think you should expect me to stay here and watch you run off to meet up with Dale tonight and be happy about it. Not when I love and need you as much as I do. So you doing it looks like you'll be ending what we once had. All to be with Dale. You wanting to go to him as bad as you seem to want to makes me feel as if we are already done. So again, take a suitcase or three with you when you go."

Lisa was scared now. She knew there was only one thing to do. She knew it was the only thing. But was she going to do it? She felt trapped, even though it was a trap of her own making.

Before she could make her decision, it was Shanty's turn to speak. "I think, Lisa, that you're not being fair to Mack. It's a simple thing. He wants you and needs you with him tonight. And there's plenty of reasons why he does. I was with him today, and in a lot of ways I have the same kind of feelings. No one should ever have go through, should have to watch, what we did today. So you damn well should do the right thing and be with him tonight. Not Dale or anyone else. He loves you more than anyone on this earth will ever love you or has ever loved you. He's not at all telling you what you can or cannot do. You getting upset because he loves you the way he does is uncalled for. You are so goddamn lucky to have him that it's impossible to describe. And you should know, there isn't a woman who knows him who wouldn't in one way or the other love to have him the way you do if their world would allow it. So get your shit together. Because one thing is for damn sure. If he splits with you, whatever he does, I will be doing it with him. Even if Kathy is then the main woman in his life. Not to mention again, that there are a whole lot of women who would love to have him. I think you forget that, Lisa. Right now, Dale's goddamn paperwork means *absolutely* nothing. Nor does whether or not you see Dale or help Dale or do anything with Dale mean shit. It sure as hell doesn't. What you are doing to Mack right now goes a long way beyond stupid. An incredible long ways."

Lisa felt as if the whole world had suddenly slammed down on her. She knew Shanty was right. Mack wasn't wrong about how he felt. All he did was answer her honestly. It wasn't okay with him for her to go help Dale. Other times it probably would have been, but not tonight. Not after all they'd all gone through that day. Not after what ever it was that had happened at the refuge. Just that alone seemed to be haunting both him and Shanty. She remembered then, all he'd lost in the past. No wonder he was shaken up from his fear for what might have happened to her. And she was going to leave him to help Dale do some paperwork. What the hell was wrong with her? Her anger and impatience with Mack was gone. It was replaced by an enormous feeling of guilt. She lifted her hanging head. the first thing she saw was Kathy talking on her phone.

"That's right. You need to stop what you're doing and come here right now. Unless you prefer to have Lisa go there." She waited a couple of minutes without saying anything else before hanging up. Not even goodbye. "Dale's on his way here."

Mack sighed heavily, then looked at Lisa. "What's your answer now?"

"To what, Mack? I don't understand."

"To you and I. What do you want to do with you and I. You were just about to end it for us. Is that still what you want?"

"Oh my god, Mack. That's the last thing I want…that I ever wanted. So please don't ask me something like that ever again. I didn't want to go help Dale for anything other than to give him a chance to spend the evening with us. I was being thoughtless and when you said it wasn't okay with you my reaction to you was stubborn and very very stupid. I guess I'm good at that. God knows this isn't the first time I've made this kind of mistake. Please, Mack, forgive me for being so totally stupid. *Again!*"

"I do. Now what else is it that you want? What are your plans for when Dale gets here?"

Before she could answer, Kathy said. "She does't have any. He's going to be real tied up until tomorrow. She's not even going to get close to him. Not tonight."

"Right," Lisa said, shaking her head at Kathy. "So is Mack going to be busy." She surprised him then and again sat down on his lap. It was something that Kathy almost always did when they got together. Lisa knew that this night, it was one thing that needed to be different. It was for Mack. She now owed him at least that much, after what she'd just put him through. She hoped it would be enough to get him through the night. She could see, now that she was finally paying attention to him, that something much worse happened at the refuge that day than she was aware of earlier. She knew she should have paid the same attention to him as he always did to her.

"Are you going to tell me, Mack, what happened at the refuge today, and what this was all about? I was too distracted before and wasn't paying attention the way I should have. It might help if you talk about it."

"Not now. Maybe later." He tried to hide them, but she could see the tears welling up in his eyes. She knew then, that what happened to him and Shanty was dramatic enough so that his concern about her shouldn't have been first. It was obvious to her now that he loved her beyond all reason.

Lisa then did the one thing she thought might help. She put her hand on the side of his face, pulling him toward her. She kissed him with all the passion she could find. It took a moment for him to respond, but when he did it was with enthusiasm. As it was their entire married life, it didn't matter what their fight was about or who started it, when it was over it ended with a passion strong enough to drive away all that was between them. She was sure they were again where they belonged. Together.

"It's about time," Shanty said. She was happy for them, even if she did have a very sad look in her eyes. With all that she had, and she had so much, the one thing she wanted most, that she'd gladly give everything else for, was the one thing she knew she'd never have. She wondered then why Lisa often didn't understand what she had with Mack and how lucky she really was. As far as Shanty was concerned, it didn't matter what evil was done in the past. Not to her, not to Lisa. What ever it was, they should be over it. What mattered was what they had now, today. She had her freedom and billions of dollars. Lisa had all that mattered, that had real value. Her life with Mack.

Kathy watched them too. A part of her she was keeping hidden from everyone, was wishing Lisa had gone to town. She loved Dale, but at this moment, her feelings matched Shanty's. Lisa might have wanted Dale earlier, but it wasn't near as much as what Kathy wanted now.

Mack's eyes met hers right at that moment. A strong shudder rolled through him. Love like that, coming from her, filled him with wonder while it also terrified him. Given the true feelings he was having about his relationship with Lisa at that moment, the look in Kathy's eyes was a truly dangerous thing.

CHAPTER 19

Lisa was the first to go to bed that night. "I'll be with you in a couple of minutes," Mack said when she went into their bedroom.

She undressed and got into the bed. She didn't bother with any kind of nightwear. She was sure that after their serious misunderstanding, there would be a lot of making up to do before they slept. It was a rather large surprise then, when he came into the bedroom fully dressed and sat on the edge of the bed.

He softly touched the side of her face, tipped his head to the side, and said, "I'll be sleeping on the couch tonight."

"My god, Mack, why the hell are you going to do that?" The tone of her voice told him that what he said made no sense to her.

"Tonight, for the first time since we've been together, I'm not sure I'm the one you really want in bed with you."

"I thought we settled that earlier. You said you forgave me for my stupid mistake, and that it was all okay now."

"I lied. It's not okay. I wanted us to stop fighting for everyone's sake. Yours, mine, and everyone watching us. Everyone there deserved better than what we were giving them. Especially Shanty. After what she went through, what she saw, and what she did, she didn't need to listen to us fight because you were having another thing about Dale."

"I wasn't having a thing about Dale. When I said I wanted to go help him, it really was just so he could spend some time with all of us. I wasn't thinking about sex at all."

"The thing is, you were thinking mostly about him. Above and beyond everything and everybody there tonight, you were thinking about him. If you would have gone, we both know it would have taken you to the next step. I don't care about the sex so much. It's where your priorities were that's bothering me."

"I don't think I had priorities, Mack. I was just being stupid and thoughtless. I was very wrong tonight. But it wasn't for the reasons you think. It wasn't because I was preferring him over you."

"You can keep telling yourself that, Lisa, but it won't change what is. I know that your feelings for him have been getting constantly stronger. You haven't hidden them at all well. I can't change that. So I have to decide if I want to live this way. I told you a long time ago about what could happen if we weren't super careful. The one thing I can't live with, is wondering every time we do something…anything, if it's me or Dale you want to be with. So I'm sleeping on the couch tonight. Tomorrow we'll decide what to do with our future. But to be honest, I don't see much of one for us right now."

Lisa wanted to answer him, but was crying too hard to do it. When he stood up to leave her, she took his hand in both of hers. Choking back a sob she said, "Please, Mack, don't walk away from me. I know I was a horrible bitch tonight. I totally understand why you feel the way you do. The thing is, will you try to find it in you to understand why I can be such an idiot sometimes. I didn't know what you'd gone through today. I still don't know what happened to you. All I knew was that Roy, Ben, and I came close to disaster and Dale pulled us out of it. Then I found out my little sister was forced to kill someone. My brain was no longer functioning very well when I decided I should go and help Dale. When I did it though, I didn't know what happened to you. Only that you were kind of worried about me. But you've been worried like that a lot of times. So I wasn't thinking about your feelings. I was only thinking about doing a simple favor for a man who saved our ass today. That's all there was to it. So come to bed and tell me what happened to you and Shanty today. I need you to be close to me now, just as bad as you needed me close earlier."

Mack didn't move. He looked down at her, wondering what he should do. He loved her. There was no doubt about that. And he did understand how she could get lost in her feelings when she decided she owed someone something. It had always been her way. But he wasn't quite ready to join her in bed. Instead, he again sat down and touched her cheek.

He swallowed hard to choke back his feelings about what happened that day. "A bunch of armed men came into the refuge," he said, staring at the floor as he talked, "hunting the bear. I wouldn't tell them where she was when they ordered me to, and they were pissed as hell. Then Teddy's father, Ralph, saw the bear and lifted his rifle to shoot it. Teddy saw it too, stepped in front of the gun so he couldn't shoot the bear. Ralph shot too quick and shot him. Shanty grabbed the barrel of his gun and pulled it out of his hands. She swung from the barrel and hit him on the head. It was hard enough to give him a skull fracture.

"Then out of nowhere another bear with four half grown cubs attacked those men. Everything went nuts then, and there was blood flying all over.

"I used a gun I managed to take away from one of them and did some serious head damage to three of them before Shanty used a twelve gauge to convince them all to surrender. The men who aren't in the hospital are in jail. It was right after that when I learned you were in trouble. I lost it then. Shanty helped me get through it. I should have been helping her. Yet she hasn't once complained, and here we are, fighting like a couple of juveniles while she's all alone. I…we haven't been fair to her. Of all of us, she's the one we should be comforting."

"I can't tell you, Mack, how bad I feel right now. I should have known what happened to you two. I should have paid attention and listened to you. And you're right, we both should be paying attention to Shanty. She shouldn't be alone. Why did you let her go home alone?"

"I asked her to stay with us. She wouldn't because she felt that it would be better for us to be alone tonight, after the fight we had. I couldn't convince her otherwise."

"That's too bad, but I think we should change that. The best thing I think we can do for her is for you to go and spend the night with her. She shouldn't have to be alone."

"What about you, Lisa?"

"Right now she's more important than I am. You said you were going to sleep on the couch. Sleeping with her isn't going to change that much."

"Wait a minute, Lisa. Even if I did go over there I wouldn't be sleeping with her. Not in the way I think you mean. I'd be on her couch instead of ours. I'm not going over there either way. If I did, she'd just be worried and fretting over you and what I'm doing to you by being with her."

"Then get her to come here."

"I already tried. She doesn't want to ever come between you and I. She's sure that if she's here, we won't makeup the way we should. I think she believes our marriage is more important than her own life is. She cares that much about us."

"Tonight, Mack, she said she would stay with you if you and I split."

"She was just telling you that she would stick by me and that she didn't think you were. She's always said that you and I belong together and that we should never let anything split us up."

"She's right. We shouldn't. At the same time though, we shouldn't leave her alone any longer. Not after what she went through today. Not with what she's probably going through right now."

"No, we shouldn't, but she won't come here even if I ask her to again. And I don't think I should go and stay with her. With you and Dale, we have enough questions already."

"No, we don't. Only you do. When I'm doing it with you, Mack, when I'm doing anything with you, I have never wished I was with someone else. Not Dale, not anyone. I like doing it with Dale sometimes, but I've never thought about that when I'm with you."

"Okay, then I'm sorry for wondering about it. I think though, we should be more careful about how we deal with things like that. Which tells me that there is no way I will leave you here alone and go to Shanty. I care one hell of a lot for her, but you come first. Even if we don't make it, I don't think leaving you here alone tonight is the right thing to do."

"I appreciate that, Mack. The thing is, she's a person who, when you think about it, matters just as much as you and I. So I still think you should go there and convince her to come here or if you can't, then stay with her. I feel like I've caused enough problems and hurt tonight. Shanty shouldn't be the one who pays for what I did. Not tonight."

"I know I can't convince her to come here. Why don't you go and stay with her?"

"If I thought I could come even slightly as close to giving her the comfort you can, I would consider it. We both know I can't. About the only thing I could do is go with you." Lisa shook her head at that thought, then looked up at Mack. His expression was one of disbelief. She decided as she looked at him that there had been way too much disbelieving that night. She grinned. "I think that's the solution. We are both going over there."

Lisa didn't wait for an answer. She got out of bed, went to her closet and found a nightgown and robe to put on. As soon as she was dressed, she took Mack's hand. She led him all the way to Shanty's house, which was next door to theirs.

Shanty answered after the second knock. She was dressed the same as Lisa. A nightgown and robe. Mack averted his eyes when he saw her. Her translucent clothes didn't leave much to the imagination. Another problem was the fact that Lisa's didn't either.

Shanty was surprised to see them. "What are you guys doing here?"

Lisa stepped around Shanty and into her living room. There was a light blanket and pillow on the couch. A book was lying open on the coffee table in front of the couch. Shanty was having trouble sleeping.

"We came to keep you company," Lisa told her. "Mack finally told me what you guys went through today. After hearing what happened, it didn't seem right to me for you to be alone. So here we are."

"I can see that." Shanty chuckled. "Can I get you something to drink?"

"Coffee would taste good," Mack answered.

"I'd like a glass of white wine," Lisa said.

While Shanty went into the kitchen Mack and Lisa sat down on the couch. Lisa was on the end. Mack sat in the middle. When Shanty returned and served them, she moved to sit in a chair.

"No," Lisa said, "don't. Sit down next to Mack. Tonight, given how all three of us feel, I think it's best if we stay close."

"I don't know," Shanty questioned, "if it's such a good idea when I'm dressed the way I am."

"I think you're dressed just fine," Lisa argued. "I'm wearing the same kind of clothes."

"Yes, but you're married to him."

"I know. Let's forget that for now. What I want is for none of us to feel alone. Sometimes being alone is okay. Tonight isn't one of those times."

"I agree," Mack said. He patted the couch next to him. "Sit down." He knew then that the two of them being there was the right thing to do.

Even though she was unsure about it, Shanty sat down. They were silent for a while, until Lisa said, "You are over dressed, Mack." She started to unbutton his shirt, the look on her face more of a smirk than a smile.

"I didn't bring any other clothes," he argued, pushing her hands away. "I'll have to keep these on." He knew Lisa was about to pull some kind of stunt and it was making him nervous.

"Not tonight you won't." She planned on unbuttoning his shirt just far enough to tease him good. The plan failed when she kept going until his shirt was off.

Shanty couldn't believe what she was seeing. Mack was even more surprised by what Lisa was doing. What she was starting was turning into a lot more than just one of her antics.

Lisa was finding it interesting. She was getting turned on by what she was doing, with none of the feelings of reservation she always had doing anything remotely like this. Her past wasn't interfering as her hands removed his shirt, then reached for his belt buckle.

Mack was feeling a bit of terror at the strangeness of what Lisa was doing. At the same time, he was filled with the wonder of the two beautiful women beside him.

Shanty was starting to smile as she untied and opened her robe.

CHAPTER 20

Mack woke up to an empty bed in a strange bedroom. The smell of coffee filtered into the room. He got up slowly, wondering what he'd be facing. Even after a full night's sleep, he was filled with uncertainty about the previous night. He was concerned mostly about Lisa. How would she be feeling about it now?

He got up and found his way into the master bath, off the bedroom. He splashed water on his face, ran a comb through his hair, and found some mouthwash. It was with a sense of trepidation that he followed the aroma of frying bacon mixed with the coffee.

He found Lisa and Shanty sitting across from each other, smiling between sips of coffee. Mack cleared his throat to tell them he was there. Lisa looked up at him and let her smile broaden.

"It's okay, Mack," she said, lightly shaking her head. She waited a moment, then told him, "It's all okay. We already talked about it. You don't need to be worried, upset, embarrassed, or anything else negative. I'm more than okay with it. What happened, what we did, what we shared wasn't a bad thing."

"Actually," Shanty said, "for me it was something very special. More than ever now, I think you two are the most exceptional couple anyone could be. What you shared with me last night went far beyond something physical. It went to the heart of love and what it should be."

Mack was still so filled with the inability to find it real, that he couldn't find any words to answer them. Lisa watched him closely, trying to decipher his thoughts and concerns. His eyes told her that he was afraid she would be upset with him for what happened.

"I'm not upset, Mack. You should remember, I started it, and did nothing to stop it." She hesitated, took a deep breath, and explained how it actually affected her, "When I started it Mack, I did it just to tease you a little bit. I thought it might lighten the mood. We'd all had such bad days and you and I had been through another fight. I wanted to start something we could laugh at. Something I never expected would happen, happened as soon as I started it. I felt as if all those feelings of not being whole, of having some part of me missing, go away. So instead of making a joke out of it so we could laugh, I pushed it into something we could share. That sharing, Mack, changed something inside me. I feel now, closer to a whole person than what I've felt since all those rapist men did so much to damage me."

"Are you sure, Lisa," Mack finally asked, "you're not upset with me? With both of us?" At the same time, he knew that if it was true that what they did during the night had helped her to further overcome the effects of her being raped when she was so young, it was an awesome thing. Not something they shouldn't have done.

"She's not upset, Mack," Shanty answered. "We've been talking about it for a while, and she's not at all upset. It's more that she's grateful for what it's done for her."

Mack looked closely at Lisa again. She loved it as his expression changed from worry and fear too curious. It was enough for her to be able to tell him the whole truth.

"The main reason I wanted us to share what we did, wasn't because I was being noble or kind to either of of you. It was simple. Once I started it, the whole thing turned me on like you wouldn't believe. And I loved the feeling of freedom it gave me. No more being tied to the expectations of someone else's ideas and beliefs. Best of all, no more of 'Why can't I???'. I loved every bit of it, and am not even in the slightest sorry we did it."

"Just so you know, Mack," Shanty said with something between a smile and a smirk on her face, "I completely agree with her. How about you? How do you feel about it?"

Mack hesitated, trying to decide if he dared to speak the truth. In the end, he knew that was the only thing he could do. "I guess I'm a typical male. I loved it. I sort of feel like I cheated on Lisa, but I can't find a way to feel bad about it. I especially can't now, since she said she liked it too. Even more, she said it helped her with what's haunted her for so long."

Lisa stood up then. "The bacon's already fried. I can make toast and eggs now, unless you'd rather eat after?"

"After what?" Mack asked.

"For someone as bright as you are about most things," Lisa told him, "you can sure be slow about others."

Shanty laughed.

Mack said, "Oh!"

Lisa took his hand and he followed her. Shanty followed them. They ate a late breakfast. The bacon was served cold.

They stayed with Shanty until late in the afternoon. When they left, Mack and Shanty still felt some of the horror from what happened the day before, but were filled with the realization that life would go on.

Mack continued to worry some that Lisa might still get upset by it all. It didn't happen. They didn't talk about it much over the next couple of days, but Lisa made it clear by the way she consistently reacted positively toward him and Shanty that all was okay. She also made it clear that he was the only one she wanted to be at all close to for a while.

They also spent most of their free time at the hospital, visiting Bob, Teddy, and Lenard. The saving grace to that was the fact that all three of them were slowly but steadily getting better.

Lisa's feelings were respected by Dale, and Kathy was busy with concerts every weekend during that time, so she didn't pay any attention to the fact that Lisa was staying closer to Mack than usual. The thing that she did notice and that did bother her some, was the fact that she missed Mack more than she did Dale the whole time she was away from home.

Mack and Shanty threw themselves into their work. It was something they needed to do to keep from dwelling on what they'd shared with Lisa.

The last thing they wanted to do was anything that might upset her. What they didn't yet realize was being reminded of that what the three of them did, gave Lisa a feeling of a new kind of freedom. She was finally rid of the shackles she carried since she was raped years before. Even so, Mack and Shanty's concern meant a lot of extra work got done in the refuge.

The volunteer kids stayed home for the rest of the week along with the following week. During that time, there were meetings held by various groups in Kingsburg questioning whether or not children should be allowed to work at the refuge. The place was still considered by many to be a dangerous place for kids to work. After all, more bears or mountain lions or wolves could show up there. Even coyotes could be dangerous as far as they were concerned.

The consensus among most groups was to simply keep the kids out of there. A couple of groups wanted to find a way to close down the refuge entirely, and in that way eliminate the chance of dangerous animals living to close to them.

The subject of land use was then brought up. Enough people believed that it was being wasted now. It should be put to direct human use. It would be okay to leave some of it for recreational use like hunting and fishing. At the same time, a lot of it could be farmed. Most important though, so much of it would make a great industrial park. That could bring manufacturing and other jobs. Something which would help speed up the growth of the entire area. Now wouldn't that be a positive move.

CHAPTER 21

They were gathered together in Silas Frederic's man cave two days after the disastrous crash of so many of them when they blindly drove into sheriff Dale Magee's trap. They were all angry, and the more they thought and talked about the people from Clayborne County, the angrier they became. They were discussing ways to get revenge against the people who lived up north in Clayborne County, who had in so many ways screwed up their lives. The worst of those offenses had ruined their hoped for championship high school football season. The newest member of the group, Ralph Tomkins, was talking.

"They're such a stupid, nasty bunch. They think even a stray, mangy dog is worth more than playing football. Them two old men, what gave me hell just 'cause I ran over one, was that way. Man, some of the things they said. I sure would like to get even with them."

"That bitch Lisa was with them too," Silas said, "wasn't she?"

"She was. I didn't see her though. She was with the stupid dog at some vet's office when them two said all of them mean things to me. I bet it cost them a lot of money to get that damn dog fixed up. It sure don't make no sense to me why they done it."

"Not a damn thing them people do makes much sense," Silas complained. "I've been checking on them. That Lisa runs a detective agency. Them two old men who gave you all that hell are her husband's uncle and father. They're the ones what were in the truck our boys was chasing the night they all crashed in the trap that sheriff set up for them. Lisa's husband Mack manages that wildlife refuge up there. He works with some broad all the time. I haven't been able to find out anything about her yet. I'm still working on it. That, and where the hell did they get all the money they needed to make their goddamn refuge so much bigger?"

"The question I have," Ralph said, "is what are we going to do now to get even? We should do somethin' to get even right now. I don't think it gots to be anything really big or nothin'. We just gotta do somethin'."

"The dog," Silas said. "Let's go to that vet's and get that goddamn dog and put a bullet in it. That will at least show them we ain't done with them yet. The bastards. After that, we got to get that damn Lisa bitch."

It took them several phone calls to various vets to find the dog. It didn't occur to them to check on the closest one first. They were just smart enough to convince the vet, when they finally found him, that they were picking up the dog for Lisa.

After they picked it up, shot it, and then to make it look even worse, gutted it, they took it up north in the middle of the night and left the body on the steps of Refuge Rescuers office.

Donna, who was the office receptionist for Refuge Rescuers, was the first one to work in the morning. When she saw the dog, she screamed so loud that both Ben and Roy heard her. They immediately left their houses at a run to help her. Roy called Mack. He and Lisa were there in minutes.

Lisa recognized the dog right away. She called the vet to find out why she wasn't notified when the dog was ready to be released. They told her what happened, but Lisa didn't think there was any excuse for their negligence. She told them that and demanded a refund for the care they'd given the dog.

She didn't care at all about the money, but wanted the refund to teach the vet's office a lesson. She was the one who brought the dog in, so they should not have released it to someone else. The vet, of course, refused to refund the money, but did give her a description of the two men who picked up the dog. She called her credit card company and let them deal with the issue. That alone would create a hassle for the vet's office. But if it didn't produce the refund, Lisa would use a lawyer or two to harass them way beyond what the refund would be.

With that done, she took the dog to the place it would be buried. Telling everyone she would dig the grave, she took a long handle spade and started. She hoped that digging it would somehow ease her anger. It didn't. With each shovelful of dirt she grew angrier.

How could anyone be enough of a lowlife to murder an innocent dog, just to get even after they lost a fight they started. Worst of all, was the fact that there were so many people who were willing to condone almost anything, up to and including the raping of innocent women and girls, to protect a total asshole just because he could throw a ball. And do it in a game?

She didn't get the chance to dwell on it though. Her cell phone rang. It was her sister, Julie, calling. "I hate to bother you," she said, "But we just found out there's a heart coming in for Dad. He's being transferred to the heart clinic in Minneapolis by helicopter. Can you give me and Beth a ride down there?"

"Of course. Where should I pick you up?"

"We're at the hospital. As soon as Dad's on his way, we'll be right out front, waiting."

Lisa found Mack and told him what she was going to do, then rushed home, took a quick shower, and put on a skirt she wore for special occasions. Sown into the back of the waist band was a special pocket. Inside the pocket, there was a switchblade knife. When the proper button was pushed, the blade popped straight out. A blade that was sharpened to surgical precision. She locked her pistol and its holster in the glove box of her pickup, knowing she'd never be allowed to bring it in the heart clinic when they got there.

When she picked up Julie and Beth, there was a sense of urgency with everything. So Lisa turned on the lights and siren, left over in her truck from when she was a deputy sheriff, so she could push it faster on her way to the clinic. She wanted all of them there before Bob went in for surgery.

She dropped Beth and Julie off at the main entrance of the clinic, then drove to the parking ramp. It was crowded and she was one floor from the top before she found a parking space. The car that followed her up the ramp found a space just three cars away from Lisa.

She wondered about the man who got out of the car and walked her way. He was acting as if he wanted to talk to her about something. Before he reached her, a second speeding car pulled up next to her. It screeched to a stop and four hulking men got out, surrounding her. She didn't hesitate, and before they could make a move on her, her hand was in the pocket in the waist band of her skirt.

She pulled out her knife, but didn't immediately pop the blade. Watching the men closely, she managed to move enough so she could back herself between two parked cars. That positioned her so the men were forced to try to take her head on, and do it one at a time.

"You might think about what you're going to do now," she told them, "because if you don't back the hell off, it won't matter how this ends. You all will, in one way or the other, pay dearly for it."

One of the men pushed close to her. "Ain't nobody payin' nothin', 'cept you bitch," he threatened. He grabbed his crotch to try to prove to her what a man he was. "And man, you is goin' to pay like you ain't never seen before. You is past due gettin' what you got comin'."

He tried to pull her out from between the cars. It didn't work quite the way he thought it would. She easily avoided his reach and caught his middle finger as his hand flew by her. She gave it a practice twist, but didn't stop it when the bone cracked, then broke. She continued the twist until a good portion of the bone was out into the open air. She followed the with two fingers jabbed into his eyes, blinding him. Then, just to emphasize to the other three men that she wasn't there to take what they thought they could hand out, she popped the blade on her knife. She made a quick slash on either side of his privates. She pushed the blade in just deep enough to draw blood. Then kicked the man hard enough in the chest to send him sprawling across aisle.

"I need to use this again," she said, holding up her knife, "and the next one of you is going to lose all of your *little* treasures."

That's when the first man who was parked close to Lisa said, "I think, boys, that you'd best listen to the lady, and get the living hell out of here. It'd be a good idea to take your buddy to a hospital somewhere. He is, after all, bleeding."

The three men were too surprised by what happened to respond right away. They stood there with their mouths open, trying to decide what to do. They were sure they should do something. They couldn't admit defeat by leaving. How could they possibly allow a woman defeat them. It would be way too much. They were real, honest to God really tough men. She was a puny little woman, put on earth only to serve and service any man who wanted it from her. Her only other purpose was kids. Making and raising them. So they were sure they needed to do something.

Lisa decided then that she'd had enough of their crap. She lifted her hands about shoulder height, moved them so the backs of her fingers were facing them, then moved them as if she was beckoning them to come to her.

"Come on, assholes. You want to get it on with me, I'm right here. Come and get me, if you're stupid enough to try. It'll be fun, cutting all your tiny little junk off. And when I'm done, I'm going to feed them to you. Right to the point you'll be choking on them."

They didn't move. The couldn't believe what she did. How could a mere woman invite all three of them to take her on. Instead of answering her request, they looked at each other, each expecting as they did for one of their friends to make the first move.

The man from the other car laughed at them, shook his head and said, "She's already got you beat, so you might as well get the hell out of here while you still can go in one piece. If you don't, I doubt like hell she's going to show you any mercy."

The three men gave each other a few more glances. Knowing they were already surely and soundly defeated they loaded their injured pal into their car and left. The man from the other car put out his hand to shake Lisa's.

Before she took it, she asked, "Who the hell are you anyway?"

He took a step back. "Sorry for not saying anything right away. My first instinct was to try to defuse the situation." He slowly reached into his pocket to take out his ID. He showed it to her. He was a US marshal.

"How the hell did you happen to be here?" She asked.

"I was already near here on a separate case when I got a call telling me to get to this clinic, and to keep an eye out for you. They sent me a text of your picture and what you would be driving, so I would know you. It was a good picture, but it was nothing to compare with real life. It's hard to believe that someone as beautiful as you could fight the way you do."

"So why are you supposed to keep an eye on me?"

"I have no idea. It all happened so fast that all I was told was to watch you. I'm sure though that it had something to do with what just went down with those men. You must be someone awful important for the marshal service to interrupt a case so we can protect you."

"I hate to disappoint you, but I'm not anyone who's especially important. I'm just here because my dad's getting a heart transplant. So I think I'd best get into the clinic to see what's going on with that."

"That makes sense, but I'll be tagging along with you."

"Why?"

"Those are my orders."

"You got some lousy orders. Mostly now it's going to be nothing but waiting. Mostly boring. Like waiting in hospitals almost always is, mostly torture."

"That's okay, Lisa. If I have to wait with you it won't be too difficult."

"I'm not all that sure where your compliments keep coming from, but I think I should tell you that I am not only married, I am probably the most married woman you've ever met. The last thing in the world I want to do now, is cheat on my husband."

The Marshal smiled. "I totally understand. I'm very much married too, and like you, I have no interest in cheating. At the same time though, you are an incredibly beautiful woman and it damn sure won't change the world or your life or mine if I tell you that. I think it kind of makes the world a little better place if we once in a while say something nice to each other. You are definitely a beautiful woman, Lisa Thomas."

Lisa could help herself then and gave him a wide smile. "And you, Marshal," she told him. "are one big hunk of a handsome man. And the damn truth of it is, if we were in a different time and place, I think it would be a special thing to get to know you better." She chuckled then, hoping he wouldn't take her comments too seriously.

"Me too," he agreed.

They stared at each other for a moment. He had a strong urge to kiss her, and from the look in her eyes he thought she might let him. Instead, he took her hand and they walked to the elevator. The touch of their hands gave Lisa a feeling she didn't expect. It was something wasn't able to feel, other than with Mack, only a few days ago. She knew then that her night with Mack and Shanty had changed her more than she realized.

He stayed with Lisa, Julie, and Beth then. It was along wait. Lisa often talked to Mack on the phone during the wait. The Marshal talked to his wife several times. Lisa and The Marshal avoided eye contact while on the phone.

When the doctor finally joined them with the great news that the operation had gone well and so far everything looked good, there were hugs all around. The Marshal got his share of hugs from all three of them, but the one from Lisa felt like something special.

Later, when everything had settled enough so Lisa felt free to leave for home, The Marshal said he would escort her to her pickup. His assignment was to stay with her until she was safely on her way. Julie and Beth were staying in the city, so it was only the two of them when they went into the parking ramp. They held hands on the way. Lisa again felt something extra from the touch of his hand.

She turned to him as they reached her pickup. "It's a strange world sometimes, Marshal. We don't actually know each other yet, but I kind of feel bad about having to say goodnight to you. It's like there should be something else, something more."

"I know," he agreed. "I feel the same way. But given who you and I are, to do anything else would probably end up with too much hurt for someone. So all I'll say with my goodnight is that for reasons I don't yet understand, I won't ever forget you, Lisa. I would tell you that I love you too, but that would be the wrong thing to do."

"It would." she sighed heavily. "But damn, life does twist us around sometimes." She sighed again, moved her hand to the back of his neck and pulled his head down to her. She kissed him and it lasted a long time. "Goodnight," she said, and noticed tears in his eyes too.

He turned and walked away from her. She knew she would likely as not see him again. What hurt was the fact that when she did, the distance between them would have to be kept great, no matter how close they were physically. She had a long ride home. It would have been a long night too, if it would have been anyone other than Mack holding her the whole time.

He knew it would be best to wait before he asked her why she was so quiet all evening, and why she was so desperate for him to hold her so tight to him now. Her quiet tears were an even bigger mystery. There was, he was sure, something new about Lisa that he would need to watch and deal with very carefully. No matter how strong she was, there was till a part of her that was fragile. A part that was his duty to protect.

CHAPTER 22

Lisa was quiet in the morning. Even when she took Mack back to bed and quickly moved over him, she did it without saying a word. After, she kissed him with a passion that was strong, even for her, before they left the bed. She remained silent the whole time.

At breakfast, she gave everyone there a brief summary of her father, Bob Anderson's, condition. She said nothing about the other events of the previous day.

When breakfast was done, she told Mack, "I need you to be with me today. I won't tell you why, but I'm afraid to go alone. And no one else but you can help my fear."

Her words shocked Mack. Lisa afraid? How could that be. She had put herself in mortal danger countless times without showing any fear. He knew something had to have happened to her that was, if not different, at least exceptional. And whatever it was, she was being truthful when she said she was afraid of it. Her basic silence though, told him it wasn't a normal kind of fear. Could it be from something inside her, rather than some outside threat?

It was an easy decision for Mack. He readily agreed to go with her, but let her do the driving. It gave him the chance to watch her, to study her face and the look in her eyes. He had no doubt that they would eventually talk about whatever was troubling her. He hoped though, he would be able to at least develop some idea of what it was before they talked.

She was equally determined to hold off showing Mack any kind of emotion that would indicate what was bothering her. It was something she was successful at until the same car that followed her into the parking ramp the previous day, again followed her.

Without realizing what she was doing, she sighed heavily when she saw the car in her rearview mirror. Mack picked up on it right away, and turned to see what was behind then. He kept his eye on the car as they left the truck, then closely watched the man from the car as he approached them.

Something seemed to flash across the man's face and stop in his eyes as he first looked at Lisa. At the name time, Mack felt a slight tremble rumble through Lisa. He turned to her. The look on her face was fear. The look in her eyes was something quite the opposite. He knew then what Lisa's problem was. He had felt the same thing a long time ago. Her name was Linda. He knew this was something that would never have a simple answer.

The Marshal put out his hand for Mack to shake as he introduced himself. Lisa kept her head down and only nodded a greeting. He returned it.

"Lisa hasn't said anything to me about you," Mack told him. "So it might be a good idea if you do."

"Of course. I've been assigned the job of guarding her while she's here. So that's what I did yesterday and what I'll be doing today. I've been told enough about you, to know you can handle about any kind of trouble that might come along. But I have to hang in here anyway. I think you know enough about law enforcement to know I can't walk away from an assignment because I don't seem to be immediately needed. The thing is, after the trouble yesterday, there's a damn good chance I will be needed."

"Something else she didn't tell me. Again, I'd appreciate it if you do."

Lisa interrupted. "Before he does, Mack, I need to tell you why I haven't said anything about yesterday."

"No, Lisa, you don't. I already know. The look the two of you have tells me. So I have two questions. How far has it gone between you, and how far are you going to take it."

"It's gone no where," The Marshal answered, "and there are no plans to take it anywhere."

"But the truth is, Mack," Lisa said, "the reason I so badly wanted you here today is because even if we already decided that we will never let what we feel take us anywhere, something could happen. He loves his wife and I love you too much to let any kind of feelings do anything to damage those relationships. I wish I could explain this. I can't. For the life of me, I don't understand it at all. I only know one thing. You and Shanty took me out of what I was. If you hadn't, this couldn't have happened."

"I can see that, Lisa. And I understand where you two are coming from," Mack said, wondering about his own mixed feelings about what their relationship might be. His own affair with Linda seemed at the time as if it was taking place in another time, in another dimension. The big difference from then to now was the fact he was single at the time. These two were both married.

"I think, Lisa, you and The Marshal have drifted into Linda's world. There's something there that is close to impossible to ignore. That means you have a huge decision to make."

"No, Mack, I don't. I can't go there. I've already done too many stupid things to you. It was just a couple of days ago I almost did it again. It was just luck and Shanty that fixed it. It changed what's inside me, Mack. The change made me strong enough to walk away from this. It's true that it is sad. We'll hurt and sometimes regret walking away. There'll be more times though, when I hold your hand, or when his wife sits in his lap, that we'll both be grateful we did. No matter, I'm glad you came with me today."

The Marshal nodded his head in agreement. "I am too, Mack. Lisa's an amazing woman and beautiful beyond belief. I will never forget and will always be grateful for the little time I get to spend with her. But she belongs with you, and it would be wrong for anyone to ever do anything to change that."

"The thing is though, Mack," Lisa said, smiling, "I need to do this." She moved into the Marshal's arms, pulled his head down to her, and kissed him. It said everything. For that brief moment, they were in Linda's world. A world free of the endless limitations ruling all of us.

It showed on the faces of The Marshal and Lisa that Mack's response to the smoking kiss was a smile. The only thing their kiss did to him was to momentarily carry him back to the time when Linda was still with them. It was a wondrous time, and a time he could never forget, even if he wanted to.

Mack and The Marshal each took one of Lisa's hands as the walked to the elevator. She no longer let her head hang in fear of what might happen. Instead she walked with her head held high, proud that she could hold two such strong hands and know that only one of them would always be there. No one needed to tell her again about how lucky she was to have Mack Thomas in her life. She would always have a memory and a spot in her heart for The Marshal, but far more important than that, she would have Mack.

Mack and The Marshal felt something special too, and because they did they were slightly less alert than normal. The two cars screaming up onto their level in the parking ramp carried eight men this time. They each had an aluminum softball bat in their hands. They all looked totally confident that this time they would win the fight.

What they didn't know, what they weren't smart enough to know, was who it was they were about to attack. They were especially stupid about Lisa. It didn't matter how often or how bad she beat them, they still couldn't comprehend the fact that a woman could. All of them had always beaten the women they attacked.

Another extremely important thing the attackers failed to take into account was the fact The Marshal was armed, and the gun he carried at his waist was a powerful semiautomatic. Lisa was armed too. She was wearing her special skirt again. It only took and instant to reach for her knife. It was in her hand before the attackers were completely out of the car.

Lisa recognized one of the men as the kid who drove the car that purposely ran over the dog they'd tried to save. She pointed him out to Mack, then gave The Marshal a quick explanation about him. All three of them decided then that if there was a fight, that young man would not walk away undamaged.

Lisa knew she wouldn't be playing any games with any of these men. She would show them no quarter. As many as she could possible take down, were going down. And she fully intended to keep her previous day's promise. Whenever it was possible, she would do what she could to destroy what ever little trinkets they carried between their legs. It made no sense at all for them to be doing any breeding. The world certainly didn't need anymore like them.

The lead among the attackers got close to Mack first. He swung his bat hard, missing Mack's head by less than an inch. It was the last thing he did that day. Mack answer the swing with a right hand under the man's chin that landed so hard he was unconscious before he even started to fall. The blow also snapped his head back hard enough to damage his neck. He would be wearing a brace there for a long time. Mack took his bat out of his hands on his way to the ground, then used in on the head of a would be football player. That was two down.

Lisa was so much faster than the first man to reach her, that it took him a moment to realize vast amounts of blood was spilling between his legs. He screamed and dropped to his knees. The second man who approached her took one look at the first man who tried to attack her and quickly backed away. Right into The Marshal who took him out with the butt of his automatic.

Mack, who had never played baseball or softball, discovered he was exceptionally good with a bat as he quickly out maneuvered and took out two more of the men. The Marshal took out the last two. Lisa didn't get the chance to get anymore. They were all so busy trying to stay away from her, that they had made it easier for Mack and the Marshal to do what they did.

When all of the attackers were safely disabled and on the ground, The Marshal made the first call. It was to the marshal's office for backup. He knew enough about the local police force to know he'd need support when they arrived. As far as he knew, they were all football fans.

They were lucky, and the support team from the marshal's office arrived before the police. They kept the hassle from the locals to minimum. It still took a few hours to get it all settled.

Bob was awake when they finally got a chance to go to the waiting area outside his room. The doctors were only allowing minimal visitation, so Mack and The Marshal just waited the couple of times she was able to see him.

As they did, The Marshal found it interesting, but also wondered why Beth spent every moment Lisa was with Bob, talking quietly to Mack. At the same time, Beth was more than a little curious about the way Lisa talked, in a voice too low to hear, to The Marshal more than she talked to Mack. Julie watched it all and knew she needed to have a long talk with Lisa sometime in the near future.

Even with those mysteries going on, it was a long day, and Mack, Lisa, and The Marshal were relieved when the day was over. As they made the journey to the parking ramp, Mack could see a deep sadness overtaking Lisa.

He had no doubts about the love she had for him, but there was also no doubt about her feeling bad about having to say goodby to The Marshal. It didn't matter to him what anyone else might think, he understood how she could feel so sad and have such deep feelings for someone she'd only known for two days. Linda taught him how that was a possible, just as she taught him that no one person can entirely fill the needs of another person. Sometimes there needed to be something more. With those thoughts, he made a decision that he consider was not only fair, but best for Lisa. After all she'd lived through in her life, she should at least be able to have this end with a good memory. Especially since, for the first time in her adult life, she would be able to.

He didn't say anything until they reached her pickup. "I'm glad I got to meet you," he told The Marshal as he shook his hand. He then turned to Lisa. "I think you should walk with The Marshal to his car and make your goodbyes there. When you do, Lisa, you take whatever time you need. I'll wait for you, and I'll love you as much as I ever did when you come back to me."

Lisa's face filled with the shock she felt about what he said. The Marshal's mouth dropped open and his head shook. He was too surprised by Mack's words to be able to say what he was thinking. Mack knew anyway.

"She won't know if you don't tell her," Mack said, referring to the Marshal's wife. "And if she knew Lisa's story, she likely wouldn't be upset anyway. Go now, and make your goodbyes. Lisa needs this."

Still not totally believing what was happening, the two of them walked to his car. Before they reached it, Mack sat down in Lisa's pickup. He had no desire to watch them any further.

Time past easily for him as he waited. He spent it remembering his times with Linda. It was enough to tell him that everything was okay, even though when she was murdered it left gaping hole in his heart. If he could live through that, he could easily live through this. Most of all, he knew this short moment he'd just given Lisa would be a memory she'd keep with her for the rest of her life.

His thoughts so filled him that he was surprised when Lisa came back. Gone was her sad, somewhat empty look. Her face carried a broad smile, and even the way she sat behind the wheel of her pickup was changed. She was more than back to herself. She seemed to be renewed. Just seeing her the way she was now filled him with good feelings.

"I have some things to tell you, Mack," she said before starting the truck. "One, that was the last time I will ever see him. He will be taken off this assignment tomorrow. He said he believes you are a decent and good man. A special kind of man. As much as that, I think you are the most understanding husband, the most marvelous man, and the greatest lover on earth. I love you so much that I don't think I'll ever be able to show you how much. I'm grateful too. I hope there's something I can do for you."

"There is."

"Oh good. What?"

"Stop in the refuge on our way home."

"Are you sure, Mack? Even after…"

"I'm sure. I love and need you that much now."

"Okay."

She stopped at the refuge and quickly drove to a special, private place to park. She knew then, that no one could or would love her with the depth Mack did. No one else would have wanted her to have what he was sure she wanted. What he was sure she'd shared with The Marshal.

At the same time, he was very much in need of the reassurance he would get from loving her. He made it clear that he didn't want to wait. She let him pull her skirt out of the way, then lifted herself up when he pulled off her panties. Without any hesitation she moved over him. Facing him, she smiled as he slid inside her. She loved the look of confusion on his face.

"It's not what you expected, is it, Mack?"

"No, I thought you went to his car so…."

"It was only to say goodbye. I did need and want to do that. I kissed him. Several times. That's all. I only knew him for two days, but there was already too much there between us to cheapen it with a quickie in the back seat of his car. In another time, place, and dimension, yes, I would have made love with him. That's not where we were, not where we are, not who we are. We are here and what's real is you and I and what we have."

"Are you sure that's what you really wanted, Lisa? I could see how you felt about him."

"What I'm sure of is that I love you with all my heart. With everything I am. The fact that I fell in love with a man I hardly know hasn't changed that. He feels the same way. His wife is, and has been for their whole life together, what his life is about. Sure, we wanted something more. I guess we are all always wanting something more. The trouble is, all too often getting that something more would have left us with something less. This was one of those. Maybe in another time and place we could have had it. Not now though. Not today. Now, today, it's time for you and me."

"Still, you could have had more, Lisa. I would still love you every bit as much as I do now. You know that what I always want first is for you to have what you want. To have what makes you happy. I didn't want to get in your way this time either."

"I know. You always do, except when I do something really stupid. Like I did when I impulsively thought it would be a good idea to help Dale with some paperwork that could easily have waited. I didn't want to do something like that again and I was afraid I might. I don't like me much when I do that. That's why I so badly wanted you to come with me today. So I wouldn't do something stupid. And if you think you were surprised that we didn't do anything when we easily could have, it wasn't near as big a surprise as the one you gave us. I know how you think because of what you learned from Linda, that there is a right time and place, just as there is more often the wrong time and place. Even so, telling us that tonight was the right time and place for us did come as a shock. The fact that you did it the way you did, played a role in our decision to not go anywhere beyond some sweet kisses as a way to say goodbye. They meant a lot. It's a hard thing, when you have to say a forever goodbye."

"You could still stay in contact. I won't object."

"No, Mack. We can't. It would be too impossible. So let's you and I do our best to forget that anything like this ever happened to me. We have too many other things to concern ourselves with. And number one on that list will be how the hell are we going to explain to Kathy what happened between you and I and Shanty."

"Are you sure we need to? Or that we even should?"

"Yes, Mack, we definitely do. We can keep today a secret. It was only us. What we did with Shanty was actually all of us. Kathy mostly, but Dale too, was effected by what you and I and Shanty did, even if they weren't there when we did it."

"I know. I'm just afraid Kathy will be hurt by it."

"Maybe. But she's stronger than you know, Mack. A lot stronger."

And with that she moved to finish what Mack wanted when he asked her to stop in the refuge. They managed to do it, but Lisa made sure that it took a long time. It was well into a star filled summer dark when they again headed for home.

CHAPTER 23

Lisa went alone to visit her father the next morning. The new marshal guard met her in the parking ramp again. Unlike The Marshal, who wore street clothes, she wore her uniform. She was in her thirties and in almost perfect condition. She was an ordinary pretty, but had the kind of figure that few men didn't notice. She carried herself in a way that told the world around her that she was no one to be trifled with.

"I'm Connie Peters," she said as she shook Lisa's hand. "I hope you and I will get along better than you and your last guard apparently did."

Lisa had no control over the deep blush that quickly covered her face from Connie's comment. She, of course, noticed Lisa's embarrassment. She couldn't stop her smile. Lisa shook her head, almost as if she was trying to rid herself of a cluster of demons.

With a telling sigh Connie said, "I kind of knew it was like that with you two. He is the kind of man who makes us all take notice. You're not the first to react to him. Don't feel bad though. He's about as married as a man could get. He's never once responded the way he could to any woman other than his wife."

Lisa couldn't help liking Connie. Still blushing, she gave her a smile and said, "I'm totally married too. It's just that sometimes nothing is what it should be. Sometimes though, it is possible to do what's right and walk away, no matter that it hurts. Maybe even a lot. He's a good man. A really good man. Like my husband, a good and loving man. We did the right thing."

Connie looked hard at Lisa then. What she saw seemed to surprise her. Lisa made no attempt to hide her feelings. She knew all along that they would somehow come out no matter what she did.

"I guess," Connie said, her smile gentle now, "you and I will never get along quite that good. I hope we can be friends anyway."

"We can be friends. I needed to be *only* a friend to someone yesterday. I can be your friend today."

"Okay, Lisa. Friends it is." She lowered her head, slightly shaking it. "It's hard, isn't it," she said, "when you have to give up such really good friends."

"Hard? Yes, it can be. Especially when you pass on the one chance to make it more while it's there." Lisa smiled. "But it's a special thing to have had someone like that, even if friends is all it was. Or ever could or should be."

Connie took Lisa's hand as an old friend would while they walked to the elevator. Lisa decided then that she would, if possible, avoid introducing her to Mack. He had enough women wanting him. He didn't need another one. Which is what he would have if they met. No matter what Connie's station in life was, Lisa was sure that with her and Mack, there would be an attraction. After all she and Mack had gone through in recent days, she was sure they didn't need to add any more complications to their lives. Especially not one like Connie.

Right at that moment, Mack would have been grateful to Lisa for her decision if he'd known about it. Since the night he spent with Lisa and Shanty, Shanty's attitude and approach toward him changed. She didn't do anything to push herself on him, but she stopped trying as hard to avoid any kind of direct physical contact. Her voice now carried a softer lilt to it, and her eyes told stories to anyone who might take the time to look into them. It was no longer her mission to avoid letting him see how she felt about him. When they were alone, she now let the obvious be obvious.

At the same time, he was haunted by the thought of the conversation Lisa wanted to have with Shanty, Kathy, and Dale. Lisa was sure, because of their relationships, they needed to be open and up front about what they did.

The idea bothered Mack because he was concerned about Kathy's reaction to it. She was already showing signs of preferring Mack over Dale. Those feelings alone could make everything far more complicated than what could be considered comfortable or safe.

He struggled to keep his thought about it to himself throughout the morning. After he and Shanty took a break for lunch, then stopped at the hospital for a short visit with Teddy and then Lenard, his thoughts on the subject eased up some.

Teddy appeared to be recovering as expected, and they had a nice talk with him. He asked about returning to the refuge as a volunteer when he was healthy enough to do so. He was delighted when Mack told him he'd be more than welcome back at any time. His mood change to one of concern though, when he asked about the bear. It worried him that she hadn't been seen since the incident where he was shot.

Mack, however, managed to lift his spirits some when he explained that it was a good thing for the bear to be gone. At least for the foreseeable future. There were just too many mighty male hunters, with a lust for killing the bear, for it to be at all safe for her in the refuge.

The last thing Teddy said just before they left him, was that his father was in jail, and that Teddy hoped he be there for a very long time. Mack totally agreed with Teddy, but only gave him a nod of his head in acknowledgement of his comment.

Their visit with Lenard was far less successful. His recovery was suddenly progressing far slower. He didn't look well at all. And the only thing he wanted to know about was Julie, and when was she going to come and see him. When Mack told him about Bob's heart transplant and how serious it was, Lenard only seemed to half understand what he was told. He again asked about Julie, and wondered why she hadn't been there to see him. Mack made a mental note then to call Lisa and tell her to bring Julie home with her, so she could visit Lenard the next day. From the looks of the man, there might not be many days left to visit him.

Lisa did as he asked. Bob was making a good recovery from his surgery, so Julie finally felt okay to go home with her. They went straight to the hospital when they got to Kingsburg. Julie was shocked when she saw Lenard. His condition had obviously deteriorated so far he literally looked to be on death's door.

Julie held one of his hands, then used her other one to touch his cheek. He was only half conscious, but he managed a slight smile when she touched him. The look in his eyes told them how grateful he was to see her. His course breathing smoothed out some as she stood close to him, holding his hand.

"I'm so glad you're here," he said, his voice barely a whisper.

"I wanted to be here the whole time," she said, "but my father had a heart transplant, so I needed to be with him. If I could have, I would have been here."

"I know, Julie. You did what you had to do. I'm grateful that you could come to see me at all. I so badly wanted to see you one more time before I die."

"*Die! You can't die!* I won't let you. You and I have to find out who we are long before you get to die. So you better just plan on staying alive until we both get older. A hell of a lot older."

Lenard's return to a recovery mode didn't happen immediately. He was in such a dismal state when Julie got there that even the doctors had slim hope for his recovery. She, however, refused to give up. She never showed, nor allowed anyone else around him to show, any negative attitudes about his recovery.

It was in the middle of her third day with him that something resembling a smile appeared on his face for a short time. It was followed by a stronger, longer lasting one a couple of hours later.

"It's about time," Julie told him. "It's what I've been waiting for. If you can smile, you can damn sure get well. From now on, that's what you're going to be doing."

"It's only because of you, Julie," he said with a voice still somewhat muted. "If you wouldn't have been here to make me believe I was going to get better, I don't think I would have made it."

"I might have helped, but you did most of it yourself. You are a strong man and you will heal now. I have more good news too. My dad's doing so good, they're letting him transfer to this hospital tomorrow. So I won't miss being with you any days until you're much better. When I visit dad, it won't be any more than an hour or two at a time."

Things settled in then. The attacks from city dwelling football fans stopped. After their last loss of eight men, three of them football players, the few left who were still hungry for revenge couldn't put together a mob big enough to dare stage any attacks. They were also having problems putting together a full football team. Too may of their players were suffering from some kind of injury they got trying to get some revenge on Lisa. As big and tough as they were, they just weren't able to defeat a small female from up north in Clayborne County.

At the same time, Mack and Lisa were getting along fine with one exception. They still hadn't come to an agreement about getting together with Dale, Kathy, and Shanty to discuss the experience they had with Shanty. Lisa very much wanted the meeting. Mack was as much worried about it as she was wanting it. Kathy was his reason. He was concerned about what her reaction to the story would be. He was sure it would be very negative.

The first Saturday Kathy did not have a concert scheduled, she insisted on having a day walking with Mack in the refuge. It was something they tried to do at least once a month, and was always a favorite kind of day for them. This time was different. Mack was nervous about it. He was afraid she would somehow sense something about his night with Lisa and Shanty.

He was, of course, mistaken. There was no way she would have normally suspected anything, and wouldn't have this time. Except for Mack's behavior. From the time they started their walk it was obvious to Kathy that something wasn't right. It only took a very short walk into the refuge before Kathy stopped him.

She looked into his eyes and said, "Okay, Mack. What the hell is it. I know you've got something bugging you. I just don't have the slightest idea what it is. I think it'd be a good idea if you told me, or else this is not going to be a good day."

"I should have known better than to think I could ever get by without telling you. The thing is, do you think it would be possible to tell you about it tonight? Lisa, Dale, and Shanty should be there when we talk about it."

"I don't think so, Mack. If we wait until tonight, this day is going to be spoiled. All I'll be doing is wondering about what the hell is going on now. After the fight you and Lisa had, any kind of secrets worry the hell out of me. Our walk isn't going to be what it should be until we get this settled. And damnit, Mack, I really do need this walk. *I need to be with you today.* Without anything hanging over our heads.."

"I understand that. We still need to have the others involved when it is explained. We'll all have to talk about it."

"How the hell are we going to do that? They're all busy doing their own thing."

Mack sighed. "That's what god made our damn *cell* phones for. I'll call Shanty and you can call Dale. Where do you want us to meet up."

"Well, I'm pretty sure this is the kind of conversation we won't want interrupted. It also seems like, still morning or not, a cold beer or a glass of wine will be a definite asset to have while we talk. So the Mystic Curve will be as good a spot as any. We aren't likely to run across anyone we know in a bar this early in the morning."

They made the calls and drove to the bar. They were the first to arrive. The place was nearly empty. A few people were scattered around at the bar and a single booth held four rather large young men. They made no attempt to hide their stares at Kathy when she walked in with Mack.

They sat down at a table large enough to seat six people and waited. Shanty got there next, and got the same stares as Kathy. Other than a hello she didn't say anything when she sat down. Mack did get a curious look from her. He shook his head in answer to it.

Lisa was all smiles when she and Dale got there. They were together because they always were on the days Mack and Kathy walked the refuge. Dale looked just as confused about the why of the meeting as Kathy and Shanty did.

Mack was the first to speak. "We are here because something happened that one way or the other either has or will affect all of us. Lisa wanted to have this meeting right away. I'm the one who put it off. We're doing it now mostly because Kathy knows me too well. She knew there was something going on with me and needs to know what it is. I'm not going to tell you though. Lisa can do a much better job of it that I can."

"Before I tell you guys the main reason for this meeting," she started, "I want to tell you a story. Mack and I weren't planning on talking about it, but I think it says a lot about a lot of things. So I'm going to tell it. It's about me, but in it's own way it's even more about Mack. It happened the first two days of dad's heart transplant. I fell in love with a man who I met for the first time the day of his surgery."

Lisa went on to tell them, in detail, everything that happened to her and how Mack reacted to it. She finished with, "So you can see from this what an awesome man, what a great and understanding husband

Mack is. How many men could love a woman so much that they would tell her she was free to say goodbye, any way she wanted, to another man she loved, even if that love was only two days old. It took an incredible amount of caring for me for him to do that. He's done that kind of thing before. When he did it this time, he gave me more love than what I thought was possible to give. More than that, he knew that something had changed inside me that allowed me to fall in love with the Marshal. The cause of that change is what we are here to talk about. Unless one of you objects to talking about it." Lisa looked at Shanty. She returned the look, smiled and nodded her head. "Before I say more," Lisa said, "I have to tell you that this wouldn't have happened if I wouldn't have been such a total idiot to Mack earlier that night."

Kathy didn't say anything, but her eyes were wide as she stared at Mack's reaction to what Lisa told them about The Marshal.

He said, "Something we all know. There's right a time and a place to do things. Just as there's as often a wrong time and place to do things. Seeing Lisa finally free of so much that has haunted her for so long, I couldn't do anything other than what I did. And from the way it turned out, what those two people genuinely felt for each other in that short time they had, I wouldn't in any way change it. That said, I think it's time for Lisa to tell you the rest of it. Just try to understand when you hear this story, the reasons it happened, and how it not only changed Lisa's life, it has made it so much better."

Lisa started the story with a brief summary of the fight she and Mack had and quickly went through the events that gave the the reason to go to Shanty's that night. She got a little of the devil in her then and took her time explaining how she undressed and seduced Mack. She then explained how many of the things that plagued her from the time she was kidnapped and raped seemed to slip away when Shanty became a part of it.

"I'm sure," she finally said, "what happened to me that night had a lot to do with what happened with The Marshal. Before then, the only men I could let close to me were Mack and Dale. I don't at all mean though, that I want to seek out other men. I most certainly don't. It's just means that it would be possible now. Before it wasn't. I feel whole, and I can breath free now."

Mack looked at Kathy, afraid of what he would see. It was the opposite of what she expected. She was laughing. "So what's is the plan for the future, Lisa?" she asked. "Is what the three of you did going to be a consistent part of what you three do now."

"Not really," Lisa answered, returning Kathy's laughter with a wide smile. "But what happened does change things. Especially for Shanty. I think we need to take that into account now."

"You don't need to do anything special for me," Shanty said. "I just want to continue to do what I've been doing. Mack belongs to you, Lisa. I won't ever do anything to try to change that. As far as he goes, I just want to keep on working with him."

"Of course you do. That's as it should be. Having you working with him is one of the best things that's ever happened to him. The trouble is, life being what it is, you being limited to that really isn't fair. Not in the scheme of things. So one of the things we should change is our attitudes. Mine already has. I think that from now on, it will be okay if once in a while I share Mack with you. I know it's up to Kathy and Dale, but I think it would be a good thing if Kathy could feel that way about Dale too. You know that the four of us have had a kind special arrangement now and then. As far as I'm concerned, adding you too it is the right thing to do. It just has to be kept to the right times and places. Most of the time, if you are with one of them, that's what it will be. Only the two of you. There might be, however, times when I might get involved. What ever else might happen, might happen."

"You have certainly given us a lot to think about," Kathy answered. "Any other time, place, or people, and I would scream such a loud no that the whole town of Kingsburg would hear me. The thing is, you are right." She looked at Shanty. "You are one of us, and I for one am damn glad you are. So, Shanty, you have a full yes from me. Now it's out of my and Lisa's hands. It's up to Mack and Dale to deal with it however they think is best. And as far as anything else, it'll be like Lisa said. What ever happens, happens."

Dale finally had something to say. "What about Shanty? Have you two taken into consideration what she might think or feel about your bright ideas?"

"Of course they have, Dale," Shanty said. "They know where I fit in here and what my past life was. What I already have here was so much better than anything else ever was in my life, that I find it impossible to explain. As far as their offer goes, it's no secret that I'm very much in love with Mack. I'll take whatever he and Lisa allow me. As far as you go Dale, I have no idea. But given the way things already with you four, I think it will be fun to give it a try. Like Mack, you are a really good man. And damnit, what ever happens, happens."

Mack couldn't help but grin when he said too Dale, "I guess you and I will just have to figure out a way to deal with this. I know it's tough," he laughed, "but we'll have to do our best to handle it."

At that, Kathy laughed too. She stood then and took Mack's hand. "I still expect at the rest of the day at the refuge with you." She looked first at Dale, then Lisa. "All the rules are suspended for the rest of this day," she told them. "I don't know what you two had planned, but I think that now, after the kind of talk we've had, Shanty should definitely be a part of it."

Lisa and Shanty blushed at her comment. Dale smiled.

Mack and Kathy made a cheerful exit. Mack knew exactly where in the refuge he was going to take her first.

Dale, Lisa, and Shanty finished their drinks before they left the bar. Because the conversations they'd had, and because they were now filled with previously unexpected anticipations, they paid no attention to anyone else in the bar. They didn't notice that the four young men in the booth, across the room from them, followed them out. The men caught up with them in the parking lot.

"That's as far as you people are going," one of the men told them. "You are all going for a ride with us." He looked at Shanty. "We know who you are. You got to be worth one hell of a lot of money, and someone has got to be willing to part with a bunch of it to keep you alive. We plan on being the people who get that money."

None of the men had yet gone beyond telling Shanty what their plans were. Lisa especially, was still standing loose and free. "I have to tell you assholes," she growled, "that none of us are going anywhere with any of you. If you were smart, which you so fucking obviously are not, you'd turn around and walk away before we hurt you the way we are going to hurt you. Especially me. I'm not going to stop with a beating this time. At least two of you are going to end up so beaten when I'm done that you will never again live a normal life. You have really pissed me off."

Having never before heard those kind of words from a woman, the four men were momentarily stunned. Their hesitation let Lisa set herself physically and put her mind where it needed to be to do the maximum damage to any would be kidnappers. She stood with her hands to her sides, but stared hard into their eyes as she waited for them to make the first move. As she did, she said, "Shanty, even if you can't take him right away, hold off the one on the left for a minute or two. Dale, take the one on the right. If you don't hurt him properly, I will when I finish with the two in the middle." She turned back to the four. "Well, what's it gonna be for you stupid and useless assholes? Walk away or the hospital?" Just to emphasize to them, what her mood was, she spit in the face of the one who did the talking for them.

She watched him ball his hands into fists and clinch his teeth. The fire in his eyes was strong when he decided he was going to hit her hard enough to make her eat her words. His wild swing at her with his right hand missed her by a wide margin, and threw him off balance. She was far faster than he was and a totally trained fighter. More than that, she new better than to give a man his size any kind of a chance if she could avoid it. She slammed her foot onto the side of his knee as he twisted around with his wild swing. It didn't break, but it did pull loose some tendons. He screamed with the pain as he fell. The second middle man thought he had Lisa now. She knew better. With no hesitation in her movement, she landed on one foot and came up with the other. It slammed into his gut. As he doubled over from the blow she slammed the palm of her hand onto his nose hard enough to smash it, rather than just break it. As he went down, she moved to finish the first man. He was trying to push himself up from the ground, so she stomped hard on one hand, then did the second one. They were both broken and he dropped down with his face in the gravel of the parking lot. As soon as he landed she used her heel to kick him on the side of the head, knocking him out. As she turned again, the second man was on his feet. He lunged at her with his hands out in front of him. There was no doubt that he wanted to grab her neck and strangle her. She decided that she'd fooled around with him enough. She kicked him, with everything she had in her, in the groin, then slammed her entwined fists onto the back of his head when he doubled over. He too, was unconscious when he landed face first in the gravel. Lisa used her foot on the back of his head to grind it just a bit harder in the rock. She looked then to check and see how Shanty was doing.

Shanty's man was on the ground, still conscious but groaning loudly. She looked down at him and said, "It's time for you to shut the hell up." The man looked up at her and groaned even louder. Shanty shook her head. "I said that's enough." He groaned one last time. Then Shanty kicked his teeth out. "He said when he came for me that he was going to fuck me until I bled. I wonder if he knows who's fucked now. He shouldn't have said that. Not to me."

Dale stood next to his man, who was lying face up on the ground. It was no longer possible to tell what his face looked like. Dale held up his hands toward Lisa and said, "I think I've been *not* nice enough to him for now. We've made our point. Kidnapping Shanty is not going to be tolerated."

Lisa nodded in agreement but did turn to the first man she fought. He was still unconscious. She spread his legs just far enough apart, then kicked him hard enough to do some serious damage. "Be best," she said, "if he doesn't do any breeding."

In a short time several of the on-duty deputies from the sheriff's office were there. The incident was written up the way it happened and the men were taken to the hospital. They were patched up, the the four of them were cuffed to their beds. They were put in rooms in pairs so only two deputies at a time were required to watch them. That made a lot of sense, since their hospital stay was going to be a long one.

Because of the severe damage to the men who attempted the kidnapping, the incident was well publicized. That was something Dale and Lisa could easily live with. It was something else for Shanty. Now the world knew who she was, what she was doing with her life, and where she lived. The most difficult thing of all was because it became a reporter's dream to get the story of why she was working as an assistant manager of a private wildlife refuge, when she was a billionaire several times over.

CHAPTER 24

Shanty's story quickly brought an endless stream of curious people to the refuge. The general public was plenty annoying. Nearly everyone who visited the refuge looked first for her. All of them had questions, the most frequent being, "How can I get rich?"

She quickly gave them all the same answer. "Have a rich father who dies young."

Her answer stopped about half of them from asking further questions. The rest of them usually had to be told to leave before their endless questions stopped.

The reporters were far worse. Once a reporter from any part of the media found her, the interrogations were nonstop. As soon as Mack and Shanty went to work, large numbers of people and reporters swarmed her. They made it impossible for her and Mack to accomplish anything. By noon, a few days later, Mack knew they weren't ever going to get anything done as long as there were so many people crowding her. He knew too, that having constant crowds everyday, would end up with serious damage to the refuge itself.

With no explanation to anyone he took Shanty's hand, pulled her up on her feet, and led her to his pickup. Before anyone in the crowd could respond to their move, they were on their way out of there. Mack did some wild driving to ensure that they weren't followed. It was almost an hour later when they arrived home.

"We can't wait for this to get any better on its own," he said. "We're going to have to do something to control the number of people we let in the refuge at any one time."

"The simplest solution is for me to quit working there. For the next few months anyway. I'm the one they're always going to be looking for. It's the money that attracts them. It's always the money."

"I know that, but is leaving what you want? You love working there. Why would you want to leave?"

"I don't want to, Mack. I just think it's the best solution to the problem I've caused."

"You haven't caused any problems. It's the overall stupidity of the human race that's causing the problem. You are one of the few super rich who is trying to do some good with your money. Now you are the one who is constantly being harassed. I'll never understand why it's this way. The good people are the ones who are respected the least."

"I'm not so sure I'm one of the good people," Shanty said, "I spent a lot of my life taking the easy way."

"I don't think you lived the way you did because it was easy. It damn sure wasn't. You did what you did because you didn't know any other way, and because the men in your life didn't allow you to learn anything different. You would have changed what you did a long time ago if you'd have known how. You've proven that just by being here and working so hard to restore the refuge. So you are definitely not going anywhere. Instead, I think we should shut the refuge down. We should only let people in for guided tours or those who deserve special permits to be there."

"The problem with it is going to be with enforcement. It will take a lot of guards to keep people out."

"I know, Shanty. Too many. What we'll have to do is catch most of those who do get in and arrest them. If we put up enough no trespassing signs up so we can, one way or the other, make them understand that it will cost them for doing it."

"That should help. It's going to take a long time to get the word out that we mean business though."

"No, it won't take long at all. You are going to have a press conference. All those reporters want to talk to you, so we'll give them a chance to do it. At the same time, we can tell the world around here what the new rules are."

"I don't know, Mack. I'm not any good at things like that. I'm afraid I'll just screw up the whole thing."

"No, you won't. I'll be right there, standing next to you. No reporters are going to be allowed to give you a hard time. Any of them get too pushy and they'll be escorted out."

"We won't be making any friends if we do that, Mack."

"No, but we won't be losing many, if any, either. The few who understand that a wildlife refuge exists first, not to entertain people, but to offer a place of protection for all native life forms which are not human. The ones who will object to the new rules the most are the ones who already either hate the idea of a refuge or believe it should be nothing more than a playground for them. A place to use their guns to kill whatever and as much as they can. Most people won't ever hear about the new rules. Nor would they care about them if they did."

"I have to tell you, Mack, I'd rather not have one. You know how uncomfortable I can be in or around crowds. I hate talking about my personal life too. I'll do it though. I know we have to do whatever we can to get better control of the human traffic in the refuge if I'm going to be able to continue working there with you. Since that's what I want most, I will do it. You have to promise that you'll be there. No matter what, you have to be there with me, next to me the whole time."

"I promise. I won't let you down."

"What's our next step then?"

"A meeting with Sue. She takes care of any and all the technical stuff. We will want the conference broadcast throughout the spoken, video, and internet as much as possible. Then we should figure out where to have it. At first I was thinking that somewhere in the refuge would be appropriate. It wouldn't. It's too open. There's too many gun happy nutcases out there to put you in such a vulnerable place."

"Do you really think, Mack, that someone will try to shoot me? Why would anyone want to do that? What have I done to make anyone hate me that much?"

"You haven't done anything. If someone did try to shoot you, it wouldn't be a personal thing. It would more likely be done by someone trying to be famous. Given the number of people with serious mental problems who own assault rifles, someone could do it for any of hundreds of insane reasons."

"What about you? If you're standing next to me, won't they be shooting at you too?"

"Most likely, Shanty, they will. We will both be wearing armor, but we don't want them shooting at us anyway. A bullet in the head can kill us every bit as fast as one in the chest."

"I hope you know that all your talk about someone shooting us is not helping to increase my enthusiasm for this press conference of yours."

"I didn't think it would. I still have to tell you any and all of the negatives about it before we do it."

"Of course you did, Mack." She kept a serious look even as she smiled at him. "That's two of the many reasons I love you as much as I do. You are always fair and honest."

"I love you for those reasons too." He paused a moment to let their conversation settle in, then said, "It's time I think, to give Sue a call and get things rolling."

CHAPTER 25

The news conference was held in the front of the Kingsburg City Hall, where so many others took place in the past. A lot of people wanted to be up on the platform with Mack and Shanty, but Mack refused to allow it. The only people up on the platform with him and Shanty were sheriff Dale Magee, two of his deputies, and Mack's wife, Lisa. He didn't want her there, but he knew keeping her away would be impossible. There was no way she would let him or any of those with him put themselves in harm's way without her there too. Because she arrived late, Mack didn't know it when one more person joined them. Marshal Connie Peters slipped into the background to avoid interrupting anyone or anything.

Everyone on stage wore body armor. Dale and his deputies were dressed in their uniforms. Mack wore the same western style clothes he always wore. Lisa and Shanty wore jeans and rather plain cotton blouses. They both wore bras, something they preferred to leave in the dresser drawer most of the time. Mack was the one who insisted they do it. He didn't want to give any reporters a subject like the lack of a bra to write or talk about. Videos of either one of them dressed that way would grab too much attention. The more the conference could be about the refuge, the better.

Mack opened crowded conference to announce the changes they made in the way people were going to be allowed to visit the refuge. He didn't get more than three sentences complete before a totally obnoxious reporter loudly interrupted him.

"We didn't come here to listen to any crap about any useless wildlife refuge. We came here to hear what Shanty has to say. So why don't you back off with your worthless rules no one cares about and let her talk."

Mack was about to answer him when Shanty moved in front of the microphones. "If you, or any of you, interrupt Mack again, I will walk off this stage and that will be the end of this press conference. There won't be another one. And which ever one of you does it, will be given a lifetime ban from ever interviewing me or visiting the refuge." She looked at the belligerent reporter, and by pointing at him to make it clear who she was talking to, she told him, "And, you, loud mouth, if you interrupt Mack or me again without being called on, you will be removed from this conference. So if you have questions for me later, you will only raise your hand. You will not speak unless you are spoken to."

The reporter started to open his mouth. As he did, he looked at Shanty, then Mack, and quickly decided it would be best to wait for a chance to ask her a question or two later.

Shanty then turned over the conference back over to Mack. Strange as it was, the media people let him finish his short talk about the refuge's new rules and regulations, and the reasons for them, without interruption. It was strong proof that they were very much interested in the reasons why a multi billionaire would want to work as an assistant manager at a wildlife refuge.

"What is the real reason you are spending time here in Minnesota?" was the first question she was asked.

"That's a simple question to answer," she said. "I'm here because I want to be. I have friends here. Real friends who accept me for who I am and as I am. They are all the kindest and most decent people I've ever known."

"You must know," the reporter claimed, "that ordinary people like the ones you claim are such good friends are only doing what they do so they can get their hands on at least some of your money."

"I am aware that it's true of all too many people, and far more than you in your limited imagination will ever comprehend. I have been rich all my life, and believe me, I can spot a scam from very far away. There is none of that coming from any of these people. For most of them, having a lot of money is *not* a good thing. It's mostly a burden. Not something they want and definitely not something they need."

A different reporter asked, "How can you be so sure you aren't just being duped by those people? What you are doing is so strange for someone in your position in life that most of us can't help but wonder about the way they are manipulating you."

Shanty answered, "I suppose you do wonder. Most of what nearly everyone does, they do for money. It seems as though almost everything done by humans one way or the other is connected to money. Hell, the only reason any of you reporters are here listening to me is because of the amount of money I have. It's just that this time, I am here for a lot of reasons that go beyond the money thing. Which brings me to this. Since none of you can get beyond talking about money, this conference is over."

"But what," she was asked by a middle age male reporter, "could be more important than money?"

"That," she answered, "is without a doubt the most stupid question I have ever been asked in my entire life." She turned her back on everyone in the media and walked away.

Mack again took over the microphone. "I hope," he told them, "That at least some of you realize how ignorant most of you have been with your questions. Shanty wanted this press conference so she could talk about her concerns over the wildlife refuge we are so lucky to have here in Clayborne County. All any of you could do was ask about her money. That got old with the first question. But it did do something for me. It gave me the idea I've needed all along to keep the refuge viable. How to raise enough money to keep it going. From now on, with the exception of people and groups who are visiting the refuge for educational purposes, we will be charging an admission fee. Hunting, especially deer hunting, will from now on be miles away from free. Any and all other fishing and hunting will require a permit above and beyond any state fees required. As I already said, there will be fees for even such simple things as hiking any of the trails. Never again will anyone be allowed to hike across country during the winter months without a special permit. Any questions?"

A lot of reporter's hands went up. Mack pointed to a slightly overweight, middle-aged female because he liked the gentle look on her face. "There are still a lot of us who are very much wondering why Shanty, given her position in life, would be spending her time working in a wildlife refuge?"

"It's simple. She's extremely concerned about the environment, and doing what she's doing is her own small way of trying to stop the rampant destruction of it."

"I think though, she could probably accomplish more by donating to some of the environmental groups. There are a lot of good ones working hard to preserve what we have left."

"The truth is," Mack explained, "she's already given more just in the past week than what most folks could give in a lifetime. Giving money is fine, but there's nothing as satisfying doing hands-on work for something you believe in."

"I hate to tell you this, Mack," the lady reporter said, "but so far the reason you've given for what she's doing just doesn't sound right."

Her comment pissed Shanty off enough to bring her back to the microphones. She nodded at Mack as she reached them and he stepped out of her way. She wasn't smiling.

"I work at the refuge because I love what I'm doing there. It beats the living hell out of running a big corporation. As far as I'm concerned, corporate life and all its business and social life sucks. I would a hundred times rather be working at something out in the woods with Mack and a bunch of kids than I would like sitting in a corporate office worrying about profit margins. What I do now has got nothing to do with money. It has everything to do with having a life. I now have such a far better life than the one I had growing up that there is no way to compare the two."

A different reporter quickly fired the next comment-question. "That's the kind of comment that makes us all wonder about what's really happening to you. We all know what a great man your father was. Just as we know that you had a great childhood. So how can you make the kind of comparison that you just did?"

"It's easy. My father was a pedophile. He started raping me when I was twelve. It continued until my husband beat me nearly to death because he thought I liked what my father was doing. Neither one of us had bothered to stop it though. We both wanted to keep the money flowing to support our senseless, stupid way of life. From the time I was born until the day I met Mack Thomas and his wife, family, and friends, the way I lived my life was stupid, useless, and extremely painful. Now, when I get up in the morning I know that what I'll be doing will in some small way benefit first, the environment, second, a lot of wild critters that deserve to have a life every bit as much as we do. And last of all, what I do is important if the human race is going to survive. And by that I don't mean that what we do will save the human race. I know it's but a very small part of what needs to be done. I also know that to get it done, it's going to take many millions of people doing their small part to keep this planet able to support us. I also know that it will never be accomplished if people like every damn one of you reporters here can't get your heads out of your asses when it comes to talking about money. Nor much good ever happen until everyone who is in my position, or even in a similar position, does more than worrying about their goddamn money, there just ain't no way we are going to make it. So I spend my days working physically hard to contribute something to life on planet earth and at the end of each and everyday I can go home and feel good about myself. That's why I work in a wildlife refuge." She paused for a moment then, looking at all the reporters. Most of them still had faces filled with the look of disbelief on their faces. "As I suspected would be the case," Shanty continued, "most of you still can't believe what I just told you. Most of you don't have the kind of minds that can listen well enough to hear what most people are trying to say. It is simple though. What I told you is what is true. What you seem to want to believe only comes from your closed minds and lack of imagination. I find that to be really sad." She turned and walked away. Lisa stepped forward and hugged her as soon as they reached each other.

As the reporters oohed and awed over what the two women were doing, Mack moved to the microphones. "This news conference is over," he said softly, and then he too turned and walked away.

As he did, two shots rang out. Marshal Connie Peters dropped down on her knees, her left arm bleeding. She continued to hold her gun in her right hand. Mack knew the shot that hit the marshal came from behind him and he spun around. The shooter was still on his feet and struggling to point his gun at Mack. Before he managed to raise it high enough another shot rang out. The bullet from Connie's gun left a neat little hole in the shooter's forehead. Marshal Connie Peters was quickly surrounded by people wanting to help her. Lisa, who would have normally been the first to aid her was for an instant stunned enough by what happened to be pushed out of the way by others there moving to assist the marshal.

She was momentarily shocked that seriously because Mack was the target of the shooter, who was one of the mighty men who had gone to the refuge that one fateful day to kill the bear. Lisa looked at the dead man, then at Mack, and finally at Marshal Connie Peters.

As she watched Connie she felt a strange sensation flow over her body and fill her head with wonder. She remembered The Marshal and suddenly knew. She would need to be as strong and understanding about Connie as Mack had been about The Marshal.

CHAPTER 26

When the reporters did their stories about the press conference, all of them featured the shooting. Several of them questioned Connie's decision to take on the shooter who was there to kill Mack. They all believed Connie's purpose there was to act as a bodyguard for Shanty. For them, it meant that she wasn't doing her job properly. A billionaire like Shanty was far more important than a rather ordinary man like Mack.

What they didn't know was that Connie was there to guard Lisa. Shanty used her influence and certain types of contributions to be able to hire US marshals for bodyguards. While they served as bodyguards, they were on a special type of leave or sometimes assignment from the Marshal's service. She was concerned about Lisa because of the football team and its fans continuing attempts to harm her, so that's what Connie was there to guard against.

It didn't matter to Shanty that Lisa's father, Bob Anderson, was now in the local hospital recovering from his heart surgery, and Lisa no longer needed to go to the cities to visit him. She still wanted that extra level of protection for Lisa.

The reason for the shooters attempt to kill Mack was to a large extent ignored in the media too. Mack didn't much care about it, but the people around him did. All of them, including all of the people in the sheriff's department who knew him, were very concerned about it.

The fact that the shooter was part of the small mob who'd already gone into the refuge to kill the bear and who weren't bothered much when one of them shot a kid, left plenty of reason for concern. There were still a lot more of them out there. All of them looking forward to the day when they could finally eliminate Mack and use the guns they loved to kill the bear. They all wanted the refuge loose and free, with none of the restrictions from the past, and especially none of the new ones.

Mack however, being who he was, was far more concerned about Connie's wound than anything connected to him. He was upset with himself for not seeing the shooter standing out among the people watching the press conference. He felt he should have been more alert to what was happening around them. If it hadn't been for marshal Connie, who he hadn't as yet met, it was very likely he rather than the shooter, would be the dead man.

As they drove to the hospital to check on Connie, and with luck be able to thank her for risking her life to save Mack's, Lisa watched him as he drove. She knew him well enough to tell a lot about what he was thinking simply by the expression on his face. She had no doubt about how concerned he was for Connie.

"Her name is Connie," Lisa told him. "She was there the last time I visited dad down in the cities. She was The Marshal's replacement. You are going to like her. A lot, probably. We talked enough so she sort of knows about what happened with me and The Marshal. She knows too, how you dealt with it. I think she admires you for the way you did."

"How did you get to know well enough to talk to her about something so personal in such a short time."

"She suspected something when he asked for a transfer and she replaced him. She hinted at it right after we met up in the parking ramp."

"How should I deal with it? Is it best if we ignore the subject."

"I really don't know, Mack. Why don't we let her take the lead on it. If she brings it up, we'll talk about it. If she doesn't, we'll let it be. The thing that matters most to me, thanks to you and caring for me as much as you do, is my not having to feel guilty or ashamed because of it. It was an unbelievable thing that happened that ended the way it should. We, all three of us, did the right thing then."

Mack answered her with a nod of his head. They were at the hospital and he was concentrating on maneuvering the ramp as he searched for a place to park. It was crowded and they were on the third level before they found a spot big enough for his pickup. The parking ramp was built at the same time as the latest addition to the hospital, so true to Minnesota form, there was a skywalk that took them directly into it. With Minnesota winters the way they were, it was often a huge convenience for visitors. In Minnesota it is impossible to beat the winters, so most people do their best to skirt around the misery of it when they can. Skywalks were used extensively for that purpose.

The men in the car following them into the ramp were less than happy about the skywalk. They were hoping to catch Mack and Lisa in a dark corner of the ramp, on a level without the walk. They wanted to tell them that it was time to totally open up the refuge, not close it the way Mack did. Those men were gun owners and hunters after all, and for them the second amendment in the constitution gave them every right to hunt and kill animals in any and all wild places. Dangerous bears were at the top of that list. They especially thought that about wild places next to a small city like Kingsburg. The men considered waiting for Mack and Lisa to leave the hospital, but decided to go to a local bar for a few beers instead. None of them had the patience it would take to wait for Mack and Lisa to return. There would be other times and places to attack them.

Mack noticed the men and pondered for a moment about what to do about them. He quickly decided to ignore them. If for no other reason than he knew their kind well enough to know if they had to wait around very long at all, they would be somewhat out of sorts when he and Lisa returned. That would put the odds even further in their own favor if there was any trouble. Regardless of what the men did, they didn't scare him. There were only four of them.

When they checked to see how Connie was doing at the nurses station, the one who met with them said right away, "You are Mack and Lisa Thomas, aren't you?"

Surprised by her question, they both hesitated for a moment before Lisa answered "Yes, we are."

"Good. The marshal is awake and is most anxious to see you. Her wound is serious enough for us to keep her overnight, but she can have visitors." She gave them Connie's room number and they were met with a wide smile when they went into it.

"I'm glad to see you're okay," she said to Lisa. "I felt guilty leaving you there the way I did." She turned to Mack. Her smile broadened as her eyes drifted slowly from his face, down his body, then back to his face. She shook her head slowly as she turned again to Lisa. "I can see just by looking at him, especially those kind, understanding eyes of his, why you feel the way you do about him."

Mack, who had only looked into Connie's eyes for a couple of minutes, was now staring at the floor. His face was slightly flushed and his breathing was slightly off from normal. Something told Lisa this would happen between Connie and Mack if they ever met, yet it still surprised her.

All she could do was wonder. First her and The Marshal. Now Mack and Connie. She searched for the right thing to say. She couldn't find it. Her eyes met Connie's, who gave a knowing shake of her head and said, "The Marshal."

Her two words made Lisa laugh. "Sure looks like it," she said.

Mack looked up from the floor. "What?" he asked.

"It's you and Connie, Mack."

"What do you mean, me and Connie? I don't understand."

"When it comes to women, you almost never do, Mack."

"I think that this time," Connie said, "he knows. He just doesn't know what to do with it. Neither do I, Lisa. I hope I haven't upset you. Feelings aside, that's where this will remain. Feelings only. We'll not be acting out on it. I have to tell you though. It's because of me as much as you two. I couldn't handle having him for only a short time. It would have to be a forever thing. And we both know that's impossible. For more reasons than you know."

Lisa moved close to her bed and gave Connie a hug. "It'll be okay. We'll all somehow make it okay."

Mack moved close the the bed. He took Connie's hands in his and gave them light squeeze. "I don't, for the life of me, have a remote understanding of what this is all about. What I do know is the simple truth that you saved my life." He gently pulled her to him and kissed her. It started with a light touch of their lips, then instantly grew into something else. When it broke, he looked at Lisa. "I'm sorry."

"Don't be, Mack. It's okay. We'll work it out."

"Maybe I should transfer out too, the same way The Marshal did." Connie's suggestion was serious, but her expression told them that she much preferred to stay on the job.

"Please, Connie, don't do that. I would like it if you stayed. I want you to."

"So do I," Mack agreed. "At least until I can show you how grateful I am to still be alive."

"Okay, I won't run off." Her wide smile said a lot.

They were all happy with Connie's decision then. Unfortunately, there was no way they could know how much they would come to wish it had gone differently.

They visited with Connie for another hour. Mack was quiet most of the time, letting the two women talk about things women talk about. Before they left her, Lisa gave her a big hug and thanked her for saving her husband's life. Mack hugged her, then tried to kiss her on the cheek. Connie would have none of it. She moved lips to Mack's and held him tightly there for a couple of minutes. Mack just shook his head when they moved apart, the look on his face all guilt.

Lisa was jealous, but did her best to not let it show. She was sure she would be wrong if she said anything negative about it to Mack. How could she, after the way Mack told she could say goodby to The Marshal.

Mack tried to tell himself the reason Connie related to him the way she did was only because she wanted them to be friends. Which would have been okay if he didn't know deep down inside that what was happening between him and Connie was more. It was one of those strange attractions that sometimes happens. And he knew, it was too strong to ignore for very long. It meant there was only one right way for him to deal with it. He needed to stay away from her as much as he could. With luck, her time guarding Lisa would be short.

CHAPTER 27

For the next week, life seemed to go back to normal. Lisa went back to running a detective agency and Mack and Shanty worked at the refuge. The refuge kids were due to return to work in the near future, because the bear, and her new companion, hadn't been seen since the mighty hunters came after her. And now lusted for the chance to kill all six of the bears.

Connie was spending most nights with Mack and Lisa. She loved the arrangement. First, it meant she was reasonably close to Lisa twenty-four hours a day, which made her feel better about her ability to act as Lisa's bodyguard. Almost as important to Connie was her being close to Mack.

She loved the way they gathered together on the deck at the back of their house every evening, with whoever it was that showed up. She enjoyed it when Kathy was one of the people there, be it alone or with her husband, Dale. He occasionally missed being there because of some sheriff thing that needed doing. At the same time, she was a jealous of the way Kathy dominated Mack's lap, whether or not Dale was there. She was sure it would be a fun place for her to sit. Which she would have if Kathyy hadn't always dominated it.

All this time, Connie was becoming more and more playful with Mack. She loved the way she could make him uncomfortable and nervous, while at the same time he liked it and was excited by it. So one evening she sat in his lap as soon as he sat down. She just plunked herself down on him without saying anything.

He was startled by her action, and left the feelings he had from it open when he stared at her. Seizing her chance, she kissed him with everything she had. He returned it. They didn't break it until Lisa cleared her throat.

"I've been kind of expecting that all along. But as you guys know, there'll be others here shortly. So unless you plan to quit what you've started, it will be best if you take it to the bedroom."

With a sheepish grin on his face Mack said, "We're done. I don't think the bedroom is a good idea right now." He was blushing deeply. It was easy to see that even though he'd enjoyed the kiss, he felt a lot guilt over it.

"I agree with Mack," Connie said. "No bedroom. Not right now anyway." She sighed heavily. She knew that the bedroom was not a place she could go with Mack. It would be wrong for the rest of the life they lived then. "But is it okay if I have his lap for a while. For some reason, I feel good sitting here."

"As far as I'm concerned, yes, you can stay in his lap. Kathy won't like it, but she'll get over it."

The only thing Kathy said about it when she and Dale got there was, "I see Mack's got himself another one. Do you think, Lisa, that he knows it this time?"

"He knows. He just doesn't know how to deal with it. We both know that the last thing he ever wants to do is anything to hurt either one of us."

"That's true, Lisa. The trouble is, it never stops a woman from falling in love with him. Connie's no different from you and I. She seems to be in love with him the same way we are. I think, before this is over, we are going to have to let them have their time. We won't lose him over it, and after what she did to save his life it's the least we can do."

"I won't argue with that. He deserves it too. He almost always puts us first. It won't hurt for us to do the same thing for him this time. He tries real hard to hold back from it, but his feelings for her are far deeper than he thinks we know."

The rest of the evening went by the same way they usually did, with the only big difference being Connie on Mack's lap rather that Kathy. Their occasional kiss did not go unnoticed either. It did, however, leave Lisa wondering what it would have been if she and The Marshal hadn't made the decision they did when they said goodby.

For Kathy, it filled her head with thoughts of her next time walking the refuge with Mack. It was unlikely, she was sure, that she and Mack would be following all the rules for their Saturday walks. The boundaries normally there would probably not be stretched. Instead, they were going to disappear for that one day.

Mack was left feeling at loose ends. For him, it was becoming more and more difficult to handle. He had, without any doubt, strong feelings for Connie. Feelings big enough to fill him with guilt. He felt as if he was being unfair to Kathy, but Lisa worried him more. She was the least emotionally secure of the four of them, and the last thing he wanted to do was hurt her.

So he was surprised when she told him when they went to bed that night. "It's okay if you spend the night with Connie. After The Marshal, I can understand how you feel about her."

Mack couldn't lie to her, so he answered, "Thing is, the same as you and The Marshal, we both know it's best not to let things go any further. I'll always care about her, but it has to stop with that. I can't let anything take even a small part of what we are away from us. If that ever happens, it will have to be you who does it."

Everyone was quieter for the next couple of days, wondering how Lisa was going to deal with the feelings Mack and Connie had for each other. She handled it well. She totally ignored it for a couple of days. On the third day, she couldn't help but notice that Connie was very bored. Nothing interesting had happened for days, and watching Lisa spend most of her time shuffling papers dealing with the agency's business held no interest for her.

Finally, after an exceedingly slow morning, Lisa suggested that she and Connie take the afternoon off and go visit Mack and Shanty at the refuge. Connie like the idea. Especially the part about Mack giving her a personal tour of. She hadn't been there yet, so seeing it sounded interesting. Even better was the idea of going on a tour of it with Mack.

Mack thought it was a good idea too, but wanted Shanty and Lisa along with them on the refuge tour. They still hadn't reached an agreement on how to do the tour when Lisa and Connie arrived at the refuge. Mack was still unsure about going on it alone with Connie, but Lisa felt strongly that Connie had earned the privilege of a few hours alone with him. Shanty wasn't as open minded about it as Lisa was, so she tended to side with Mack.

After listening to both sides of the debate, Connie made the final decision. Two things brought her to the conclusion she came to. First it was about Lisa. She was there as her bodyguard and she felt she would be shirking her duty if she went off with Mack and left Lisa unguarded. Second, she realized that if she was alone with Mack for any length of time, the chance of them carrying things too far was too great. As much as she might desire to do that, she couldn't do it. In the short time she'd known them, she was already very fond of everyone of his people. Even the ones she'd only seen during the breakfasts at Ben and Theresa's she'd eaten with them. As much as all that, she had serious commitments of her own. So Lisa relented and the four of them made ready to go on the tour. Only the seating arrangements were different from normal. Connie would ride up front with Mack and Lisa would ride in the back with Shanty.

That's when life changed. As they walked to the four wheeler with seating for four, they suddenly heard the sound of several men pushing hard through some nearby brush. They were all armed, most of them with AR15s. One man in the lead raised his rifle, aiming it at Mack. Connie saw him first and jumped in front of Mack as the man pulled the trigger. The bullet hit her in the chest. She had neglected to wear her body armor that day. Mack went down with her, trying to cover her body from further bullets.

Lisa drew the semi-automatic from the holster she always wore. She fired blindly at the men until her gun was empty. At the same time, Shanty picked up the twelve gauge pump shotgun kept in the same shed as the four by four and she too emptied it into the group of thirty-two men, all of whom were too shaken by being shot at to return fire. When the smoke cleared eighteen of the men were running away as fast as their legs could carry them. Of the fourteen other men, ten were dead and the other four were wounded seriously enough to not be any danger to anyone.

Mack was on the ground, holding Connie. "No," he cried out, "goddamnit no! Not again. Not again." Tears streamed down his face as he held her, rocking back and forth. He stayed there, holding her until he was forced to let her go. He said on the ground then, tears running quietly down his face. He stared up at the sky and remembered. Too many had been lost to him. It was more than he take.

Lisa and Shanty stayed with him, sitting on either side of him by his truck. It took him a couple of hours before he could pull himself together enough to move. Lisa held on to him when they moved. Shanty held his hand.

When he finally managed to talk, the first thing he said was, "At least this time I could say goodby. Something I never got to do with the others." The others were women in his life who had been murdered. Then he cried again. Lisa held him. Shanty had to be the one to tell Dale what happened.

His questions for her were minimal. The AR15s littering the ground were evidence enough of what had gone down. There was little more needed after Shanty told him what happened. It only took a short time for Dale to let Shanty rejoin Lisa and Mack. They left for home then, but Mack was too far out of it to do anything but lie down when he got there. Lisa spent the night on the floor next to the couch where he slept. Shanty spent it on the floor a few feet away.

Several times during the night Mack cried out. Each time it was the name of one of the women he had loved and who was murdered. The last dream occurred just before he woke up for the day. Her name was Linda. "I should have listened closer to her," he said as soon as he sat up on the couch. "But at least I got the chance to tell Connie goodby. It should have been more, but at least I got to do that this time."

"I'm so sorry, Mack," Lisa said, "so, so sorry."

"What's worst of all, she did it for me. Why the hell would she do that. I should have taken that bullet, not her. It's not fair. Twice she saved my life, and now she's gone. One way or the other, every goddamn one of those bastards still alive is going to pay for what they did."

"I know, Mack," Lisa agreed. "They will. Each and every one of them will pay. And I will be right at your side when they do."

"So will I," Shanty, who was still there and listening to them said. "So damn well will I."

CHAPTER 28

Mack's thoughts stayed with Connie. It seemed as though there should be some way to bring her back. He knew it was impossible, but he desperately wanted to see her again. He finally gave up and decided to go to the morgue so he could. He knew it was a morbid thing to do, but he needed to somehow find a way to deal with her death. He hoped this visit would do it.

Lisa refused to let him go alone. Whatever happened, whatever he did after he saw her again, she didn't want him to do it alone. Shanty went along too. If for no other reason than to help Lisa if she needed it.

It was a sense of trepidation that they followed the man from the morgue to the room Connie was in. Someone else was already there, they were told. But they would be allowed to view the body along with the other person.

He was a big man, but his head was hanging low as they approached him. His shoulders were trembling slightly as they did. Seeing that, they hesitated for a moment before moving any closer. Mack was the first to move next to the man.

Before he could say anything, the man lifted his head. His eyes met Mack's and the two men hugged each other. The man was The Marshal. "She was my wife," he said. "Connie was my wife."

Lisa moved into his arms and kissed him. "I'm so sorry," she said. "We didn't know."

"You weren't supposed to. Connie took my place because after I told her about you after our first day together, she was real curious. I was there the second day because it took a while to set it up for Connie to take my place as your bodyguard."

"She knew all along then," Mack said, "about what happened between you and Lisa."

"She did. So she was doubly curious when I told her what you did for Lisa and me. She thought you were some kind of awesome man."

"She was the awesome one," Lisa said. "She saved Mack's life twice."

Mack choked up then, so it was a struggle for him to talk. "She died taking a bullet that should have hit me. She jumped in front of me. If I could fix it, I would never let her do that. It would be much better to have been me instead of her."

"No, Mack, it wouldn't have. It would only have been better if it wasn't either one of you." He paused, then said, "I'm Tony Peters by the way. I don't think I ever did get around to properly introducing myself those two days we had together."

Shanty took his hand and shook it. "I'm Shanty, and the truth is, what happened is more my fault than Mack or Lisa's. I'm the one who hired you guys. I've done a lot of wrong things in my life, but I'll never feel as bad about any of them as I do this one."

They first told Shanty that there was no way she should in any way feel guilty. They talked then, about Connie mostly, until it was time for her autopsy. They then decided to go to Katy's Kafe for coffee and maybe try to eat. They didn't get that far. A woman, holding the hand of a four year old boy, stopped them as soon as they got outside. She was at one time pretty, but it was hard to tell now. Her face was a mass of bruises, as were her arms.

"Is one of you Lisa Thomas?" the woman asked.

"I am," Lisa answered.

"I was told that you sometimes help women who get beat up by their husbands. Do you?"

"I do. Did your husband do that to you?"

"He did. Yesterday."

"Why?"

"He was upset about something that happened at the wildlife refuge. He went there with a bunch of other guys. All of them had their precious AR15s with them. When he came home, he didn't have his gun any longer. He'd actually shit and peed his pants too. When I asked him what happened this is what he did to me. I'm afraid to go home now."

"That's okay," Shanty told her, "you're not going home. You're going to the hospital."

"I can't," she agued. "We don't have any insurance."

"No problem. It will be taken care of. So don't argue."

"Before you go," Lisa said, "I need to know your name, your husband's name, and your address."

"Are you all going to go after my husband?"

"Let's just say this," Lisa said, "Your husband will never beat you again. In the end, the least that will happen to him will be a lifetime in jail."

"I don't want you to worry about that either," Shanty said. "I promise you that you will get through this okay."

The woman nodded in agreement, then gave Lisa the information she wanted. Shanty took her to the hospital in Mack's truck, with the agreement to meet later at home. Mack, Lisa, and Tony decided to skip the stop for coffee at Katy's. He gave them a ride home, where they invited him in for coffee and to get even better acquainted.

By then, Lisa was getting agitated from thinking about the woman and the man who beat her up. She hated him for that alone, but the fact that he was among the cowardly AR15 owners who murdered Connie gave her a lot more reason to hate. Watching the two men with her trying to deal with Connie's death brought the hate welling up inside her to the point she had to do something.

She didn't drink much coffee before she knew she was going to do what she knew needed to be done. She stood up and said, "I can't let it go. I'm going to pay that useless son of a bitch a visit. It's time for payback to start."

Mack knew immediately that there would be little he could do to stop her. Not without a serious fight. He also knew she was right. She did need to go. She just wasn't going to go alone.

"Okay, Lisa," he said, "but I'm going with you. I'll let you deal with him as long as you are safe doing it."

"I'd rather go alone, Mack. He's a wife beater and he was with the man who shot Connie. He deserves what you know I'm going to do to him."

"I'm not arguing that point at all. I only want to go with you to stay sane. If I let you go alone, it could easily drive me insane with fear and worry. I can't take the chance of losing you. You know where I'm at right now. So I have to go with you."

"I'm going along too," Tony said. "Like Mack, I won't interfere with what you do as long as you aren't in any real danger. And like Mack, I can't lose any more right now. I have to know you are safe. I will also make a couple of calls to ensure that things are taken care of when you finish with him. We won't be getting any police involved."

Mack and Tony walked with Lisa to the front door when they got to the man's house. He didn't answer it, but Lisa wasn't one to give up so easily. They went around to the back of the house. The man was talking to another man. They were lounging in a couple of Adirondack style chairs and enjoying a beer.

"You are right, Joe," the wife beater said to his friend. "It would have been better yesterday if we would have shot back. Next time, we better plan on killing the whole bunch of them Thomases and their friends."

That was enough for Lisa. She used her hands to tell Mack and Tony to stay where they were, then joined the two men in the back yard. "Well, tough guys, why don't you start your killing with me right now. I'm right here waiting for you useless, slimy chickenshit cowards to beat me the way this asshole did to his wife yesterday."

Lisa smiled, then lifted her hands in the air with the backs of them facing the two men. She wiggled her fingers, inviting them to get up and try to do something to her. Even as stupid as they were, they were smart enough to see that she had absolutely no fear of them. Something that filled both of them with fear.

It was enough to keep them in their chairs. They didn't move. She did. Up on the deck. She didn't fool around. She slapped the wife beater across the face several times. He wet his pants. She did a quick spin and raised her leg high enough to kick the man named Joe in the face. He spit out a couple of teeth. She continued to work over the two men until they were lying on the deck in their own blood. It would be a long time, she knew, before they got out of the hospital. If that's where they went next. It wouldn't have bothered her to know that neither of the men were ever seen again by anyone who knew them.

Tony never did say where they ended up. All Mack and Lisa knew was that neither the Kingsburg police department, nor the Clayborne County Sheriff's department were ever called. No one ever found a record of them visiting any hospital either.

When Tony was asked if he knew what happened to them his answer was simple. "They killed Connie."

Later that day, when Shanty returned home, Mack told her that the wife beater had been visited. When she was told it was Lisa who did it, all she said was, "Good. He had it coming."

That evening, Dale and Kathy joined them on Mack and Lisa's deck. As it always is in situations like that, talk was difficult. Dale however, did have something he very much wanted to tell Mack. He just wasn't sure about telling him in front of Tony. So he asked Mack if they could go someplace to talk in private.

Tony spoke up first. "I know enough about all of you to trust you to do the right thing. Right now, the right thing is to catch every damn one of those men who killed Connie. What happens to them after they are caught isn't necessarily going to be a problem for the sheriff's department. So if what you want to tell Mack happens to be something not quite what you'd normally do, the secret is safe with me. They murdered my wife for absolutely no reason. They should never have done that. They will pay for it. I, for one, do not plan to rest until they do."

"Okay," Dale answered, "I get your point. I have the names of several of the man who were at the shooting but who ran away. They were so scared when they did, that a lot of them dropped their AR15s when they ran. All I had to do is check the registration to find out who the extra guns belonged to. All I ask is you make sure the list of who those men are remains here." He handed Mack the list.

There was no lap sitting that evening. The sense of loss they were all feeling was too great to make any attempt to do anything that might seem to lean toward something romantic.

Lisa did, however, move to a chair next to the one Dale was sitting in and motion for Kathy to sit next to Mack in the love seat. She took his hand and held it. Only now and then did she give it a light squeeze.

Shanty sat in a chair facing Tony. She spent the whole time letting her eyes roam between Mack and Tony. When the evening ended she smiled and said to Tony, "I think it would be best if you don't try to drive any place tonight. I have a spare bedroom. You should sleep there. You and Mack are close enough to the same size, so I'm sure he'll lend you something to sleep in tonight, and fresh clothes to get you started tomorrow."

"Normally, I would turn down your offer. But things are different now, so I accept it with many thanks. It will be a good thing to get an early start tomorrow. It's always best to start a hunt the first thing in the morning."

"Good, and I want you to know. If the nightmares get too rough and the loss you are feeling is unbearable, you can always come to bed with me. I promise, I won't do more than try to fill your lonely places."

"You're a beautiful woman, Shanty, but it will be a very long time before I'll be able to do more than hold on to you or any other woman. I loved Connie more than anything, even life itself. So for now, I am useless as a man."

"No, Tony, you are not. You are still as much a man as you ever were. You will heal. You will always love and remember Connie, but you will heal. So will Mack."

Mack didn't say anything. Not even goodnight. Thoughts of Connie filled his head as he slowly walked into the house. He was forced to walk slow. He couldn't see very well. His eyes were too filled with tears.

Although it was nearly impossible for her to do it, Lisa waited until she was alone on the deck before she went inside. She found Mack curled up on their bed, still dressed.

"I can't stop remembering what happened to all of them," he said, then went quiet.

Lisa laid down and pressed her body against his back. She was still there when morning came.

CHAPTER 29

Mack spent a fitful night, often waking Lisa, so neither one of them felt particularly fresh when they crawled, still fully dressed, off the bed. Mack put on the coffee and was almost done with his first cup by the time Lisa got out of the shower.

He playfully tweaked her nipple as she did, and it sent shivers up her spine. It was such a totally unexpected thing for him to do, given the circumstances. It was still a very welcome thing. For him to be feeling as lost and empty as she knew he did, it meant a lot to her that he would take the time too, in his own small way, say I love you, Lisa.

She kissed him lightly in response and said, "I love you too."

Mack surprised even himself when he said, "If there was more time this morning, I would be showing you how much."

Lisa looked at him and knew he was telling the truth. She felt proud that she could still do that to him. Especially in a situation like the one they were in.

Reluctant as they now were they went ahead and did what they needed to do. Mack took a quick shower and as soon as they were dressed they walked to Shanty's and knocked on her door. Her and Tony were already dressed, so the four of them walked too Ben and Theresa's for breakfast.

Tony was unsure about the whole thing, especially when he saw how many people were already sitting at the table that filled the dining room of the house.

Lisa took the time to introduce everyone to Tony, but didn't bother to explain who Tony was. They all already knew. The introductions were followed by a somewhat uncomfortable silence for a couple of minutes. True to form, Roy was the one to break it.

"So, Mack," he asked, "What have all of you got planned for today?"

Keeping his face deadpan, Mack answered, "We are going to hunt down and beat the living hell out of and possibly kill a whole bunch of men."

That wasn't quite the answer Roy was expecting, but when he picked up the expression in Mack's eyes, he realized that Mack had just answered him with the complete truth.

Roy know there were a lot of things he could or should say. Instead, he answered Mack with a truth of his own. "Do you need any help?"

That broke the ice. Mack was met with a chorus of volunteers. Everyone was willing to put their life on hold in order to assist Mack, Lisa, Shanty, and Tony go after the men who murdered Connie. None of them had known her long enough to know her well, But they all knew her well enough to have been fond of her.

Tony was shocked by the way everyone responded. They left no doubt about how they felt about Connie, and every bit as much, how they felt about what was done to her. At the same time, he knew that he and Mack had to be the primary actors in the scenes to come. So he answered all the comments and questions.

"I appreciate all your offers," he said. "A lot more than I'm going to be able to tell you. But this is something Mack and I have to deal with. What needs to be done is going to be decidedly unpleasant, so it's best if we do it."

"I too appreciate them," Mack said, "but Tony's right. We are the ones who need to do what has to be done."

"The thing is," Lisa added, "no matter how they do it, Shanty and I will be part of it. There is no way they are going to do it all alone. We were there. We saw what happened. We will be there when those men get what they have coming."

Wanda then reminded them of one important fact. "If there is at any time going to be any accurate shooting involved, don't forget me. Given what those bastards did, I'll be there if you need me."

The rest of the meal settled into normal conversation then. Tony left the table with a very positive impression of everyone he met that morning.

The four of them spent some time then, going over what they were going to do next. Mack suggested that they split up. He thought Lisa should go with Tony, since she knew Kingsburg and the rest of the county the better than Shanty. He knew it well too, but Shanty was only somewhat familiar with most of it. There were no arguments over that arrangement.

Mack and Shanty's first stop was at the home of man who made his living as a custodian at the high school. He worked nights, so Mack's fierce knocks on his door woke him up. He answered it wearing sweat pants and a tee shirt. His hair was a mess and his eyes were blurry. He was home alone. his wife worked for a large insurance company down in the cities.

"What the hell do you want?" He growled. "It better be important, because you damn well woke me up."

"We want you," Mack answered. "You were one of the men who murdered a friend of ours at the refuge, and we are here to make you pay for it."

The man's face filled with fear and he swallowed hard to get rid of the bile rising up in his throat. "I ain't never murdered nobody," he whined.

"You were there," Mack told him, letting his rising anger with the man show. "You left your AR15 behind when you ran off."

"How could you know that?"

"I was there," Mack lied. "I saw you drop it."

"You couldn't of seen me. You was on the ground with that bitch who was there."

As soon as she heard the word bitch, Shanty moved in close and slapped the man several times. He was spitting blood when she stopped. She then spit in his face and followed that with a hard right hand to his gut.

"That woman was our friend," she said. "You call her a bitch again, and I will goddamnit to hell kill you." She hit him again. "Are you hearing me?"

"Yes," he gasped, "yes, I do hear you. But I didn't murder her. I never fired my gun. I didn't do nothin' wrong."

Mack grabbed him by the hair and yanked his head back. "You were there, so you are every bit as guilty as the bastard who shot her. Now, I'd just as soon as not kill you right here and right now. But I'm not going to. Instead, I'm going to give you a chance. First, you are going to give me the names of every man who was there when the bunch of you murdered our friend. If you refuse, I will kill you. With my bare hands. A little at a time. After I get the names. All of the names, I expect you to be packed and ready to leave town by the time it's dark tonight. If I see you again, I will kill you, the same as I will if I don't get my list. You won't see me coming, but it will happen."

"But my wife? She can't leave that way. She won't want to leave. Do you really expect me to move without her?"

"I damn sure do. I have to spend the rest of my life without a friend you murdered. You can damn well live without your wife. You have a choice. Leave or die. That's the price you are going to pay for committing murder. Just consider yourself lucky for this chance. You won't get another one."

"Oh my god," he whined again, "I guess I should have listened to her when she told me that owning a gun like that could never bring any good to my life. Only harm."

"She was right, asshole," Mack said. "You should have damn well listened."

The man started packing as soon as Mack left. When he was done, he spent a couple of hours writing a note to his wife explaining what happened and where he was going. He left before she got home that night.

When she did, she read his note, shook her head and threw it in the garbage. "I told the jackass," she thought, "not to buy the gun. I told him even louder to not go to the refuge that day. But would he listen. Hell no, not mister macho man with his bright new AR15, which he lost when he ran away when the shooting started. So if he thinks I'm going to follow him, he is truly out of his mind. Besides, now that he's gone I can tell my boss that I will have dinner with him Friday night. Lord knows, he's asked me often enough. And if he wants to go dancing or whatever after, well hell, I can do that too."

She did all three.

CHAPTER 30

A small, middle aged woman answered the door when they rang the bell at their first stop. Lisa's first impression of her was that she was a mousey kind of person. She held herself in a scrunched position that went along with her grey streaked hair, which was up in a tight bun. She wore no makeup and her clothes appeared to be designed to hide any figure she might have had. Her arms showed traces of past bruises.

Lisa told her who they were looking for.

"That's my husband," she answered, her voice not much more than a whimper. "What do you want him for?"

"He was there at the wildlife refuge with a mob of other men who murdered this man's wife. She was my friend. I was there when it happened. We want to talk to him about what he did."

"Oh, my," she whined, "you aren't going to hurt him are you?"

"That will be up to him," Tony told her. "You can tell us where he is, or we can go into your house and search it until we find something that tells us."

The woman cringed from his words. It was obvious from the look on her face she knew what they were talking about, and that she was afraid of what might happen. Either to her or her husband.

"He's at work," she said. "He doesn't like it if I call him there, so it's better if I don't. Maybe you should come back tonight. He should be home by nine o'clock or so. He always stops for a few drinks before he comes home."

"Where does he work?" She told them. "I think it will be best if you call him. Tell him that I said I would beat the hell out of you, the way he does now and then, if you didn't call him. Then tell him to come home right after work. No stopping for drinks tonight. We'll be here to see him when he gets home." He looked into her eyes so she could see he meant every word he said. "Do it now so I can see you do it. I'm not in the mood to wait for you to do it. I want to go to the refuge as soon as possible, to see the place where my wife was murdered."

The woman called her husband. "The first thing she said to him was, "Don't yell at me. They made me call you so I could tell you to come straight home from work. They want to talk to you tonight." She paused, then looked at Tony. "My husband wants to talk to you."

"Not on the phone. We will see him when he gets home tonight. We are going to the refuge now. Tell him he'd best be home on time tonight."

Tony touched Lisa's elbow, indicating that it was time to leave.

"I know you have something planned," She said, "but if we'd have stayed there we might have been able to learn more from his wife."

"We probably could have, but I was more interested in laying a trap for him. I'm pretty sure he'll be looking for us in the refuge. Since no one is working there right now it's a real private place. When he gets there, we will be ready for him. Call Wanda and tell her to meet us there."

"Do you plan on having her just shoot him? I want the bastard as bad as you do, but even I think a sniper killing might be going a little too far."

"It would be. I only want Wanda there to cover us from being victims of a sniper killing. This particular bastard is a wife beating drunk who I am a good ninety percent sure is a bully and a coward. He'll be bringing friends along, and if they decide to shoot us from a distance, it will be good to have a backup who can shoot as well as you say Wanda does."

"How many men do you think he'll bring with him?"

"No more than three or four. We aren't giving him enough time to be able to convince any more that that to go with him. If there's too many, we'll be forced to shoot them. But four or less, and we'll just beat the living hell out of them."

"Then what?"

"We'll have to wait and see. Worst case, they will all disappear, along with all evidence that we ever saw them."

"Sounds good. If it's possible, I'd as soon be the one to tangle with this wife beater too. I have a special place in my heart for men who in any way abuse women."

"I understand, Lisa. Shanty and I talked a fair amount last night. She told me about what the two of you went through as kids. So it's not hard for me to let you have at 'em when it comes to those men. I only ask that you don't get so angry when you deal with them that you make some kind of mistake. If you were to get hurt in any way serious, or much worse, if we lost you, it would be devastating. I love you, you know, so I don't know how I could live with it. As far as Mack is concerned, I think it could easily kill him. He's already had too much for one man to deal with in his life."

"I know. I live with it. And I don't want to ever do anything to hurt him. So I will be careful. At least, as careful as one can be in a real fight."

Wanda was already there when they got to the refuge. They found a spot at the top of a grassy knoll with a clear enough view to make it unlikely that anyone could get into a position for a sniper attack without her seeing them. And that's all she would have to do. Once she knew their location, if they made any move to shoot, she would take them out. Wanda was one of those rare people who just didn't miss.

When the man they waited for arrived, he did it without a sniper. He arrived in a Jeep with three other men. Of the four, one was of average size. The other three were big. They averaged somewhat over six and a half feet tall, and at least two hundred fifty pounds each.

They got out of the Jeep loaded with confidence, and made a big show of how confident they were. All four of them started to pound their right fist into their left hand, just too illustrated to Tony and Lisa how macho and tough they were. They were sure that by their actions, they were going to put the fear of God into the two trouble makers. Lisa spoiled their fun. She laughed at them.

"So," she said, "all you chickenshit assholes think you can intimidate us. I've got news for you. You don't. You can't. Now which one of you is the coward who dropped his gun when we started to shoot at you."

None of the four answered her. Instead, they stood there with their mouths open, two of them drooling as they did. She stepped up to the biggest of the men and slapped him across the face. Her hand was open, but the force behind the blow was enough to snap his head to one side. He reached out to grab her. She was too fast and as she moved out of his way, she kidney punched him. When Lisa took on a man twice her weight and a foot taller she didn't consider fighting what they thought of as fair. She fought to beat them.

"Before I knock you out," she asked, "are you the one I want?"

"No, but it doesn't matter. Female or not, I'm going to make you wish you'd never done what you just done. Then I'm going to spend the rest of today and all night tonight doin' to you the only thing you are good for."

The other three men decided then that it would be good idea to help Lisa's opponent finish the job. Especially now that he'd given them the idea of what they could be doing with her later. It was their fatal mistake. Neither Tony nor Lisa were in the mood to fool around with any of the men.

As soon as the average size guy realized they didn't have any chance to win, he backed up to the Jeep, reached inside it, and pulled out a forty-five caliber, semi-automatic hand gun and pointed it at Lisa. He never pulled the trigger. A high caliber bullet from a bolt action rifle pierced his forehead. He dropped his gun on his way to the ground. The other three men turned to run, but two more bullets in the ground in front of them stopped them.

"We ain't really part of this," one of the men complained. "We was just helpin' out a friend. He was the one you all wanted. Not us."

"The fact that you came here with him says something else," Tony told him. "You were here to help a murderer get away with murder so you all are as guilty as he is."

"Hey, wait a minute. Even he wasn't guilty of no murder. One of the other guys done the shooting."

"How do you know that?"

That's when the man made his fatal mistake for himself and the other two with him. "I know, 'cause I seen him do it."

"You were there? You saw the shooting?"

"Yeah, well sure. All of us was. We all seen who done it."

Tony looked at Lisa, a smile forming across his face. "The motherlode," he said. "This couldn't have worked out better. Do you have any rope in your truck?"

"I do."

"Enough to tie all of these guys?"

"More that enough."

"Good. Let's tie up these three morons. Then I've got a call to make."

When they finished, they left the three men on the ground, securely tied tight enough to keep them from any movement. The dead man was left where he fell.

Tony asked Wanda if she was okay. She pointed to the dead man. "The world's a little bit better place now. So yes, I'm fine. A lot better than I'd be if I hadn't been here. So what's going to happen to those other three?"

"Nothing we have to be concerned with. Soon they'll be in a better place."

"They're lucky," Lisa said. "Whatever happens to them, it won't be as bad as what I wanted to do."

The next day when Mack and Shanty checked out that spot, it was impossible to tell that anyone one was there the day before. Even the grass Wanda was lying on was now upright again. There was nothing on the media about the disappearance of four men.

CHAPTER 31

The hunt for the men who escaped the refuge after the murder of Connie continued until there were none left to hunt. Tony stayed with them, sleeping at Shanty's, for a couple of weeks after it was over.

What Mack noticed most during those weeks was how Lisa reacted to Tony. He knew she was strongly attracted to him, but she avoided any kind of physical contact with him. He, in turn, did nothing to change the way she was acting toward him. They both knew that it was best for everyone if they avoided even the appearance of something between them.

Their days were spent trying to live as normal as they could, given what they did for a living. Lisa concentrated on managing her detective agency, Refuge Rescuers, and Mack and Shanty worked every day at the wildlife refuge.

As Tony was getting ready to leave for the airport on his last day with them, Lisa finally relented and kissed him goodby. The instant they broke it she turned and walked away from him. Mack was the only one who noticed the tears on her cheeks. She seemed to be back to normal when he returned home after dropping him off at the airport. Shanty wasn't, and she cried most of the way home.

The kids returned to the refuge to work, and within a month most of the restoration work was done. It was late on a Friday afternoon, after the kids were on the bus on their way back to town, that Shanty told him the news he hadn't expected to ever hear.

"As you know, Mack," she told him, "I've kept in contact with Tony. He asked me to visit him. I'm going to. I'll be leaving on Monday."

"Are you coming back?"

"I don't honestly know. It'll depend on how it goes. No matter what though, I'll always be there for you, if you ever need me. For you and Lisa and all the rest of you. And if I don't come back to stay, I'll always want to visit now and then."

"I don't know what to say. I wish you well, no matter what you decide, you know that. And I'll damn sure miss working with you every day. Of all the people I've worked with in my life, you have been best. As great as dad and Roy have always been, you were even better."

"I can only say the same thing about you. I need to tell you too. No matter what I do or where I stay or how I live, I want you to know that I love you Mack Thomas. And that has a lot to do with why I'm going. As much as I care about Lisa, it's getting more difficult to stand back and watch you two, knowing I can never really have you."

"Like I've said before, Shanty, a different time, a different place. Without all the ifs and maybes involved, I would have been more than happy and proud to have you as my lifetime partner."

"There's something else you need to know. You probably won't like it much, given your strong aversion to things like this. But I've set up a special kind of trust fund for you. It's in your name only, but it automatically goes to Lisa if anything should happen to you. I've done this to you because you have a sixth sense when it come to people who deserve to be helped when they need it. You also seem to know the best way to help them. I want you to feel free to use the money however you think is best."

"You know that I don't feel all that comfortable with things like this. For you, I'll accept it, but I don't like it so much. I have a couple of questions. First, what do you want to do with your house?"

"I'll keep it. I will need a place to stay when I come to visit. And when I'm not here, you can feel free to use it as a guest house for anyone who needs a place to stay."

"Okay, we'll take care of it for you. Now for the big question. How much money did you put in that *special* trust fund?"

"Less than I probably should have."

Mack frowned at her. "Come on, Shanty, how much is less than you probably should have put in it?"

"Just a billion."

"You what? That sounded like you said a billion. You did mean a million, didn't you?"

"No, I said a billion. I want you to be able to help those people you run across in your life who need and deserve help without having to think about what's left. But if it's not enough, I can easily add to it."

Mack stared at the ground and thought about it for a while. He was smiling when he looked up at her again. "I won't tell you what I'm going to do yet, but because of this, you've helped me make up my mind about something. If I can't tell you about it before you go, I'll call you as soon as I can tell you."

They went home then, and told Lisa what Shanty was planning to do. She wasn't at all happy with it. Neither was anyone else. Everyone wished her well, but they all expressed the hope that she would return.

Mack kept quiet about Shanty's trust fund and his future plans. He planned to tell Lisa everything, but wanted to wait until he was sure it was going to work.

When the evening was over and everyone was gone, she took Mack into the shower with her. After, she put on Mack's favorite nightgown, but rather than take him to bed she took him outside and to Shanty's. As she and Lisa planned, she was waiting for them. The spent a long, but fruitful night.

Mack spent the weekend at home. He wanted to be as close to Shanty as he could, for as much time as possible, while she was still with them. Monday came way too soon for all of them anyway. It was a long, sad trip to the airport, and an even sadder trip home.

Lisa didn't argue when Mack dropped her off, saying he had a couple of errands to run. One of them was a visit with Dale at Katy's Kafe. It was afternoon by then, but they both ate breakfast. Of all the food served there, the best was their hash brown potatoes with a couple of over easy eggs, along with an order of some kind of meat.

They had a productive talk and came to a mutual agreement on something Mack was very concerned about. When they did, Dale's smile was even broader then Mack's.

"So," Dale said, "What's next?"

"Tomorrow Kathy and I are going to take an extra walk in the refuge. I'd appreciate it if you don't tell her anything before then."

"I won't. And when you tell Lisa what you're going to do tomorrow, tell her that her and I will be spending Saturday together."

"I will. And likely as not, Kathy and I will have another day in the refuge then too. With the changes coming, I'm sure she'll want one."

"More than likely. Is there anything else you've got planed I should know about?"

"Just one other thing. I'm going to be contributing, anonymously, a little money to the sheriff's department's widows and orphans fund."

"Okay, Mack, what the hell is a little money?"

"It'll only be about a half million."

"You're shitting me. That's not a little bit, Mack. That's a whole lot. Can you afford to give away that kind of money."

"Don't worry about it. I can't tell you the story. Not yet anyway. All you need to know is that it will have no ill affect on Lisa and I."

Mack's contribution left Dale real curious, but he knew Mack well enough to not push him for answers. Mack didn't say anything to Lisa concerning it. Instead they talked more about his planned day with Kathy. She wasn't surprised by the fact they were going to spend a day together in the refuge. She was only wondering why they were going to do it on a week day. They'd always spent their refuge days together on a Saturday.

Lisa's other big question was, "Are you guys going to be making love tomorrow?"

"I haven't planned on it. I damn sure won't so much as kiss her, if my doing it is going to bother you."

Lisa shook her head. "I think I asked that wrong. I'm not at all upset that you might. Actually, I think you should. Kathy's been feeing a bit left out of it for a while. I think she needs for you to love her."

Mack wasn't expecting Lisa's reaction. "I kind of figured you would prefer we stayed away from that for a while. Especially after the way you did with Tony."

"It was totally the wrong time for me to do anything with Tony. Crazy as they were, our feelings were too strong to act on so soon after he lost Connie. No matter what, I don't ever want to do anything that will jeopardize what you and I have. Anything with Tony at that time might have. He could have too easily forgotten who we all are."

"That makes sense. But with all that's been going on, why aren't you worried about Kathy and me?"

"Because with you two, you've already a long time ago gone beyond what you should have. If you were going to let it screw up our lives, you would have already done it. So we might as well all try to be happy with who and what we are."

"You make a lot of sense sometimes, Lisa. Even so, I do promise you that if anything does happen, it won't be me who starts it."

And it wasn't. It was all Kathy. However, once it started he didn't fight it much, if at all. After the first time, as they lay in the afterglow they felt, Kathy asked him, "What are you going to do now? Are you going to keep on working full-time in the refuge, or are you going to manage Refuge Rescuers again?"

"Neither one."

"Really? What are you going to do then? Take that dream trip you've talked about so many times before? You know, Lisa's never going to want to do it."

"I know."

"There's something you don't know though. If you decide to go anyway, I want to go with you. No matter where, how far, or for how long. I don't ever want to hurt Dale or Lisa, but if that's what it takes to not lose you, I will."

"Well, for now at least, you won't have to do anything quite so radical." He then told her his real plans. "I'd appreciate it if you'd keep it to yourself for now. I want to wait until Saturday night to tell her. She's less likely to argue with me after she has a full day with Dale."

"She does like those days, doesn't she?"

"Yes. We can't complain though. We for sure do get plenty to like out of ours."

"That we do, Mack. That we do."

They didn't get much walking in that day, but when Saturday came around it was a much more normal walking day. They only stopped twice. When the day was over and they had their after Saturday visit, Lisa had a couple of questions for Mack when they went to bed.

"All three of you seemed to be kind of on edge tonight. Is there something going on that I should know about?"

"Actually, there is."

Lisa knew then that something was up. Mack was going to change something, so her question now was what and how much. Or was he going to do something that could be a disaster for her. Like maybe go on that trip he so frequently talked about. She hoped not. She didn't want to leave all she had, just to travel and take pictures and write about what they saw.

"Okay, Mack," she finally said, "what the hell are you going to do now? I know damn well you're up to something."

"Are you sure you want to know?"

"Of course I want to know. If you are going to leave me, I at least want the chance to say goodby."

Mack knew he shouldn't do it, but he couldn't stop himself. He chuckled. "I can tell you had a good day with Dale," he said. "Any other day and you'd be really upset if you thought I was going to leave you."

Her face suddenly fill with her most serious expression and tears started to form in her eyes. "Are you really going to leave me Mack? Why?"

Mack put his arms around her and held her. "Don't cry. I didn't mean to make you cry. I'm not going to leave you. Not for any reason or anybody."

"Then what is it? What are you going to do?"

"It's not that big a deal. The refuge is going to need someone trained to do the job of managing it. Now that the restoration is near completion and Shanty's gone. I don't want to manage it. As far as Refuge Rescuers is concerned you are a much better manager than I could ever be. You're a better detective too. So I'm going to go back to the job I used to do. I'm going back to work for Dale. I'm going to be a deputy sheriff again."

"*Really!* That's what you're going to do?"

"It is, if it's okay with you?"

"Oh god yes, it's more than okay. I was so damn scared that something serious was wrong."

EPILOGUE

The police chief of a Minneapolis suburb, which had planned a their high school having a championship season, had four visitors one afternoon. They arrived in a rather large, black SUV, with windows tinted so dark it was impossible to see inside it.

Their clothes were tailored to fit near perfectly, but not good enough to hide the fact that the weapons they carried in their shoulder holsters were quite large. During their visit with the chief, it was suggested to him that it would be a good idea if all the football players and their fans stay completely the hell out of Clayborne County, located up north of his suburb. One of the men also mentioned that any repercussions that might follow any unwanted visits would not be official. They would simply happen.

As they left, they told the chief that they wished him good luck with their football season. It wasn't to be though. Due to so many injuries to nearly every player on the team, they ended with the worst season they ever had. They lost every game.

*****

The cop, Silas Frederick thought that his man cave in the basement of his house was soundproof, and therefore a safe place to talk about things he didn't want his wife to know about. He knew she was smarter than him. He just didn't know how much smarter she was.

The first day he was at work, when his man cave was finished, she installed microphones in several strategic locations he never checked. All conversations held from then on went to two different recording devices. She always knew from then on what he was up to.

What she especially hated was his comments to other men and high school football players, about their sex life. To get even, she cut back on that part of her life with him, and frequently shared that part of her life with an accountant she worked with. She also started some investments she didn't tell Silas about. She knew it wouldn't take more than two or three years to have enough money secretly invested to start the divorce proceedings.

*****

Quarterback Jerry Smith never played football again. his knee didn't heal properly and he always walked with a limp. After he lost his hero football player image he lost his confidence, and became unable to do anything with women. His equipment stopped working and pills didn't do him any good. He lost his scholarship, so missed going to college. He lost all interest in staying in any kind of condition and his weight grew to three hundred pounds. He now works for a puppy mill and cleans dog kennels for a living.

*****

US Marshal Lenard Shultz recovered from his bullet wounds, but took a couple of weeks leave after he left the hospital. He spent as much of that time as he could with Julie. He was lucky, and got even more time off than would be normally available. Since her sister was manager of the detective agency where she worked, she got extra time off too.

All that time off however, spent with a US Marshal, got her interested in becoming one. So she decided to go back to school to get the education she needed to apply for the job. She and Lenard also became engaged, with plans to wait to get married until she completed her education.

*****

Bob Anderson also made a full recovery from his hospital trauma. He healed completely from his transplant surgery, and at the time he was released from the hospital there was no sign of his body rejecting his new heart.

Best of all, about two weeks after he got home, for the first time in a very long time, Beth fell asleep one night with a big smile on her face. Bob was a happy man too.

*****

Mellisa Carpenter was found to be cancer free after a grueling series of chemo and radiation treatments. During her ordeal, she talked to Beth several times. She cheered loudly when the football team lost their last game, just as she had all their other games. Something she knew she would forever do every time that team lost a game.

*****

After a while there were reports of several men missing from Clayborne County and the surrounding area. As a general rule, most of the men were anything but popular, and since there was never any sign of any kind of violence connected with their disappearance, the local police didn't take it too seriously. The US marshal service didn't find any evidence of any kind of wrong doing either. Neither the local sheriff's office nor the FBI were ever called in to investigate.

*****

Teddy returned to the refuge with the other kids shortly after Shanty left. He was sorry to learn that she was gone, but still glad to be able to work with Mack and the rest of the kids. On his third day back, they all got a very special visiter.

She come out of the brush slowly, looking around as she did. She greeted Mack first, by putting one paw on his shoulder and pushing her nose into his face.

She seemed momentarily somewhat lost as she looked around for Shanty, but then returned to herself when she spied Teddy. She gave him the same treatment as Mack got, then moved to each of the kids. The best any of them got was a slight poke in the stomach from a cold, wet nose. When a couple of them reached out to pet her, she stood still for them, smiling.

It was then that Mack noticed who was watching them. She and her four cubs stayed in the brush, but did little to stay hidden from his view. He wondered then, if all of them were going to turn out as friendly as the first one to visit them. If they did, he knew it would be an ongoing problem to keep them safe. There were simply too many hunters around who were more than anxious to be the ones to do the killing.

No matter what though, he found it awesome to have another full grown bear interested in what they were doing with the refuge. Especially one with four cubs.

*****

Mack had finished the basic training of the new refuge manager and was picking up the mail after his third day of his new but old job as deputy sheriff. He didn't bother to look at it, and left it on the kitchen table for Lisa to check when she got home.

When she did, he gave her his usual greeting of a meaningful kiss, then sat down with a cold beer. He nearly fell out of his chair when Lisa screamed as loud as she did. He thought it was the loudest, most excited sounding *yes* he'd ever heard.

He got up and ran into the kitchen to see what she all the noise was about. Lisa was now standing there with a huge smile on her face but huge tears running own her cheeks. She held an envelope in one hand and a single sheet of paper in the other. She gave Mack the paper. It only had two short sentences on it.

It said, "I hope you haven't closed up my house too tight. I'm coming home." Shanty.

Mack immediately called her and told her how happy they were with the news. Then he asked her why. He had her on the speaker phone so Lisa could hear her answer. "You, Mack. You're the reason. It's all about you. And Lisa, if you're listening, don't ever forget just how damn lucky you are."

"I know I am. But no matter how you look at it, you have to admit, he belongs to you too. So hurry home. We have all missed you."

Even Kathy was happy when she got the news.

No matter what else, Shanty was one of them. This was the home where she belonged.

*****

Mack and Lisa were relaxing with a beer, out on their deck. Lisa's cell phone rang, and when she saw who was calling she left her chair and walked to a far corner of the deck from Mack.

Her conversation on the phone was in muted tones, quiet enough so Mack couldn't hear her end of the conversation she was having. From the look on her face, he could see it was serious one. It left him curious. Who was she talking to that she didn't want him to hear any of it. She talked for twenty minutes. Her face was flushed and she avoided looking into Macks eyes when she sat down again.

He knew something serious had just occurred between Lisa and whoever she was talking to, but decided not to question her. If she thought she needed to keep her conversation a secret, he wasn't going to push her, or even ask her, to tell him about it.

Mack didn't have to look at Lisa to know she was uncomfortable with the silence hanging between them. She was waiting for him to ask about the phone call. Something her obvious discomfort told him she wanted to talk about it. At the same time, he wasn't sure he did. Her reactions were telling him she was going to ask for something he wasn't prepared to give her. Especially since he had been able to pick up on a few words from her talk on the phone. The most important one being the name Tony. Mack was sure it was Tony who she talked too. He didn't think their conversation was going to bring him any good news.

After another ten minutes went by, Lisa couldn't wait any longer for Mack to say something or ask her anything. "Why aren't you asking me who called?" she finally asked him.

"I figured that if you wanted me to know, you would tell me. And to be honest, I doubt that whatever you have to tell me about your conversation with Tony, it won't be good news to me. I don't want to go through with you what we've gone through in the past. So let's not have a fight. What ever it is, I won't stand in your way."

Lisa sighed heavily as she listened to him. She knew what he was talking about, and couldn't blame him for reacting the way he was. Tears rolled out of her eyes as she thought about what he was going through again. She knew then that she should have kept her conversation with Tony in front of Mack. Trying to keep it from him was the wrong way of dealing with what Tony called about.

"You are right about it being Tony who called," she said. "And you are right about why he called. He did ask me to come for a visit."

"How long does he expect you to stay?"

"He said for at least a long weekend. A whole week would even be better." She blushed deeply and shook her head. "He said if I came and things worked out for us, he hoped we could make it permanent. He was hoping I will leave you. He said it was because you have Kathy and Shanty. With Connie gone, he no longer has anyone."

"When are you going?"

"He wanted me to come this weekend. He thought you might approve of it, after the way you let me tell him goodbye. He thought I should leave here Friday morning and come back Tuesday afternoon. But even better, it would be Monday of the second week. before I leave him."

"Which is it going to be, Lisa. The weekend, the week, or permanent?"

"What do you think, Mack?"

"If you go, I'd guess permanent. You know the why of that."

"I do. But before I give you a direct answer, I have to tell you something. I think you are the most decent, the most generous, and the most understanding person anyone could possibly be. When I think about what you did in that parking ramp. When you told me I could go with Tony to his car and take whatever time I needed to tell him goodbye. It was hard for me to believe that you could be so understanding. It still is. Tony thought so too. But now that he's lost Connie, he believes it's only fair that you at least share me with him. Giving me up would be even better. He's really lost without her. He does need someone."

"I figured that as soon as I knew it was him you were having such private conversation with. Ultimately though, it's entirely up to you. I know you care deeply about him, so you going to him isn't a complete shock. You might not mind leaving me so much, but there is a lot here you will be sorry you gave up. And I'll miss you. A lot. I hope you know that."

"No, Mack, you won't. I promise, you definitely won't miss me.."

"I will. How could I not. I love you."

"I know you do. I can't forget either, how you always say you won't get in the way of what I want. The thing is, you are all wrong this time about what I want. The reason I kept my conversation with Tony private is because I was telling him goodbye. You let me do it however I wanted to the first time I did, so I thought you would be okay with me doing it again. In private. Saying a final goodbye to someone you care about isn't an easy thing to do. But I once again wasn't paying enough attention to you to remember that you would take it the wrong way. I'm not going to see him for the weekend or any other time. I'm not ever going to go see him. I told him that the only thing for us to do was to bring our relationship to its final end. There's only one complete love in my life, and that's you. He will have to somehow find his own way to recover from the loss of Connie. I can't do it. There's no way I'd take the chance of losing you by spending a weekend, or any amount of time, with Tony. No matter how bad we all feel about Connie. One more thing. I will never again wonder about who I am. I know now. I am a whole person. All the wondering because of what happened to me in the past are gone. More than anything, I am your wife. That's the best thing of all. It's truly what I've wanted to be since the first time I ever saw you."

Mack didn't try to find the right words to answer her. His feelings were too strong to allow him to talk. Instead, he took her in his arms and kissed her with all the love he had for her. It was a kiss she would long remember. She pushed him away after, then took his hand. He followed her into the house. They were late for breakfast when morning came.

9 781961 254985